LAUREL AND THE SPRITES' MISCHIEF
by Cassie Kendall

There's great excitement in the Dappled Woods. All the signs point to it being a year when new woodfairies will be born. So the fairies are busy with preparations for this rare and wondrous event.

But then the usual peace of the woods is disturbed by a series of mischievous pranks. At first, everyone blames Laurel. After all, she *has* been known to act in an unfairylike manner before. However, when a mean trick is played on the Eldest, everyone knows Laurel can't be behind it.

Then the magical fairy dandelions disappear! Without them, new fairies cannot be born. So Laurel enlists the help of her pixie friend, Foxglove, to track the dandelions. And they are joined by an unexpected volunteer.

But even with two helpers along, Laurel doubts her chances of success. Especially when she hears that she might find more dandelions in the most dangerous part of the forest.

Stardust Classics Series

Laurel

Laurel the Woodfairy
Laurel sets off into the gloomy Great Forest to track a new friend—who may have stolen the woodfairies' most precious possession.

Laurel and the Lost Treasure
Laurel and her friends join a secretive dwarf in a hunt for treasure.

Laurel Rescues the Pixies
Laurel tries to save her pixie friends from a forest fire that could destroy their entire village.

Laurel and the Sprites' Mischief
A terrible threat to the future of her people sends Laurel on the trail of some mysterious mischief-makers.

Alissa

Alissa, Princess of Arcadia
A strange old wizard helps Alissa solve a riddle and save her kingdom.

Alissa and the Castle Ghost
The princess hunts a ghost as she tries to right a long-ago injustice.

Alissa and the Dungeons of Grimrock
Alissa must free her wizard friend, Balin, from an evil sorcerer.

Alissa's Tournament Troubles
Alissa tries to find a way to undo her own magic spell before hearts—and heads—are broken.

Kat

Kat the Time Explorer
Stranded in Victorian England, Kat tries to locate the inventor who can restore her time machine and send her home.

Kat and the Emperor's Gift
In the court of Kublai Khan, Kat comes to the aid of a Mongolian princess who's facing a fearful future.

Kat and the Secrets of the Nile
At an archaeological dig in Egypt of 1892, Kat uncovers a plot to steal historical treasures—and blame an innocent man.

Kat and the Missing Notebooks
In sixteenth-century Italy, Kat's hopes to apprentice a young artist to Leonardo da Vinci are endangered by a spy.

Design and Art Direction by Vernon Thornblad

This book may be purchased in bulk at discounted rates for sales promotions, premiums, fundraising, or educational purposes. For more information, write the Special Sales Department at the address below or call 1-888-809-0608.

Just Pretend, a Kid Galaxy Company
Attn: Special Sales Department
One Sundial Avenue
Manchester, NH 03103

Visit us online at www.stardustclassics.com

Laurel
and the
Sprites' Mischief

by Cassie Kendall

Illustrations by Robert Rodriguez
Spot Illustrations by Michael Jaroszko

Stardust
CLASSICS

Just Pretend, a Kid Galaxy Company
Attn: Publishing Division
One Sundial Avenue
Manchester, NH 03103

Stardust Classics is a registered trademark
of Kid Galaxy, Inc.

First Edition
Printed in Hong Kong
05 04 03 02 01 00   10 9 8 7 6 5 4 3 2

Publisher's Cataloging-in-Publication

Kendall, Cassie.
   Laurel and the sprites' mischief / by Cassie Kendall ; illustrations by
Robert Rodriguez ; spot illustrations by Michael Jaroszko. --1st ed.
p. cm. -- (Stardust classics. Laurel ; #4)
   SUMMARY: Signs indicate that new woodfairies will be born this
year in the Dappled Woods. But someone is playing tricks which
threaten to jeopardize the wondrous event. Laurel and her pixie
friend, Foxglove, set out on a journey to make things right.
LCCN: 99-71561
ISBN: 1-889514-29-2 (hardcover)
ISBN: 1-889514-30-6 (pbk.)

1. Fairies--Juvenile fiction. I. Rodriguez, Robert, 1947- ill.
II. Title. III. Series

PZ7.K333Lad 1999   [Fic]
                                    QBI99-662

Contents

CHAPTER ONE

Signs in the Meadow

o, Foxglove. I told you I can't go. Not now."

Laurel put down her basket of flowers and pushed back her hair. She gave a deep sigh, stretched, and shook her wings.

"All right," said Foxglove. "I thought it was worth a try." The pixie got up from the log where he'd been sitting. "It's been a long time since we went adventuring, that's all. And you said you'd finished the spring planting."

"We have," admitted Laurel. "But there's a lot more to do. For one thing, I have to help take care of Moonlight Meadow."

"I'd think the meadow could take care of itself," Foxglove complained.

Foxglove wasn't ready to give up. Laurel was his favorite scavenging companion. Until now, it had always been pretty easy to convince her to go adventuring. Most woodfairies hated the idea of leaving their peaceful home in the Dappled Woods. However, Laurel wasn't like most woodfairies. She usually welcomed adventure and excitement.

Laurel shook her head. "Not this year. I've told you that things are different. All the signs point to this being a spring when new woodfairies will be born. That hasn't happened since the year I was born."

She gazed off in the direction of the meadow. "It's really

wonderful to see. The fairy dandelions have started to grow. They're five times the size of a normal dandelion, Foxglove! The flower heads are so heavy that they almost touch the ground. And at night…"

She trailed off, thinking of what she'd seen. So Foxglove asked, "What happens at night?"

"It's like the Elders always said it would be," answered Laurel. "There's a golden glow hanging over the meadow."

"Could be swamp gas," grumbled the pixie.

"Foxglove!"

"Okay, okay," Foxglove said. "So it's not swamp gas." He shook his dark hair out of his eyes. "I know your dandelions are rare and special. And I can see why they're so important. But I was wondering…"

"What?"

"Well, are there tiny baby fairies inside the dandelion flowers right now? I mean, if I picked one and opened it up, would I find a fairy?"

Laurel was practically speechless. She sputtered, "Of course not! Anyway, how could you even think about picking one of the dandelions? That's awful! If you did that, a wood-fairy would never appear from that dandelion!"

"I wasn't actually going to do it," Foxglove protested. "I was only wondering, that's all. It does seem a pretty strange way to be born, you know."

"For a pixie, maybe. Things have always been this way for fairies."

Foxglove looked thoughtful. "How do you know the new woodfairies aren't already in there?"

"I just do," replied Laurel. "The story is told over and over in our Chronicles. When the special dandelions bloom, we know it's time for new fairies to be born. Our dandelions grow slowly—not like regular dandelions. So we tend them until the full moon. That's when they finally open. And when the moonlight strikes them, new fairies appear. I can't explain it any better than that. It's magical and beautiful and glorious!"

Foxglove shook his head. "Well, I can't compete with 'glorious.' So I give up. For now." He picked up his scavenging bag. "I'll put off my trip for a while and hang around home. When you're free, send Mistletoe or Chitters to Old Warren with a message."

Laurel gave her friend a grateful smile. "Thanks for being so understanding. I'll let you know as soon as I can go," she promised.

Foxglove started off, then paused. "Someone's coming," he said.

"I don't hear—"

At that moment, two small forms darted from the bushes. They slid to a halt at Laurel's feet.

"Mistletoe! Chitters!" cried Laurel. "Where have you been all morning? Foxglove was asking about you."

"We've been with Ivy," chattered the chipmunk. "In the clearing. That's where."

"Now Ivy's on her way here," added Mistletoe the mouse.

Laurel and Foxglove turned to see a sweet-faced fairy making her way down the path.

"Foxglove! It's good to see you," Ivy called.

As she drew nearer, she added, "So this explains why you didn't show up at the clearing, Laurel."

Laurel put a hand to her mouth. "Oh! I forgot!" she cried. Then she frowned at Foxglove. "See—I told you I had lots to do."

"I'm afraid she's right, Foxglove," Ivy said with a smile. "In fact, I'm here to ask her to come to a meeting."

Foxglove grinned. "I get the picture. I was just saying good-bye. Remember to let me know when you're ready for a bit of excitement, Laurel."

He waved to the two woodfairies and headed off into the trees.

As the pixie's merry whistle faded in the distance, Laurel turned to Ivy. "Does the Eldest want to talk to us again?" she asked.

Lately the young fairies hadn't been having their usual lessons with the mistresses. Instead they'd been spending a lot of time with the Eldest, the oldest woodfairy of all. She had been talking to them about how their lives would change when new woodfairies were born. Almost ten years ago, Laurel, Ivy, and their friends had been the last group of young woodfairies to appear. They'd never witnessed the birth of new fairies. Now the Eldest was trying to prepare them for this remarkable event.

"No," said Ivy. "The Eldest and the mistresses have gone off, just like they said they would. They're talking about the new fairies. When their lessons will start and things like that. So we won't see them for a few days. We're on our own."

"Then who called the meeting?"

Ivy shrugged. "Primrose did."

"Of course," Laurel said with a sigh. Naturally, Primrose considered herself the perfect choice for leading the younger woodfairies. After all, everything about Primrose was perfect. Her hair always fell into place without brushing. Her music was never out of tune. And without fail, her dresses were neat and spotless.

Laurel, on the other hand, was far from perfect. Her curls were usually a bit on the wild side. Try as she might, her flute often scritched and scratched on the high notes. And her dresses...

Laurel sighed again and picked at a grass stain on her sash.

"Give her a chance, Laurel," said Ivy. "After all, someone has to organize things. We have a lot of responsibility while the older fairies are busy."

"I know," said Laurel. "And I don't care if Primrose is in charge. She's good at that kind of thing. It's just that she's mad at me most of the time."

"Well," replied Ivy slowly. "You *did* hide her paintbrush during art class the other day."

"Only after she hung my wet painting on the drying rack—upside down."

Ivy tried to hide a smile and Laurel laughed. "All right. So it looked the same either way. I'm still sure Primrose did it on purpose. So I had to get even."

"What about last night? When you stuffed moss in Primrose's flute."

"She deserved it!" Laurel protested. "She kept sniffing while I was singing. Besides, it was funny to see Primrose puffing away at her flute. Her face got nearly as blue as her dress. And all you could hear was this little squeak."

Ivy shook her head. "I'm sorry I brought it up. Anyway, we'd better go. We're late."

So the two set off for the Ancient Clearing. When they arrived, the other young woodfairies were already seated on the soft grass that carpeted the area. Only Primrose remained standing. Her foot tapped a slow, steady rhythm as Laurel and

Ivy approached.

"Thank you, Ivy," said Primrose in her most proper voice. "Now maybe we can start."

She gave everyone a stern look, then continued. "As you all know, we have more responsibilities now. The Eldest and the mistresses have gone off to talk about the education of the new fairies. They'll be away at least three days. Meanwhile, it's up to us to tend the dandelions. We also have to make head-wreaths and flower garlands for the newborns. And we still have our regular duties and lessons. So I've made a few lists."

Of course you have, thought Laurel.

Primrose began reading. "Violet will gather fresh herbs. Ivy and Daffodil are to clear dead leaves from Moonlight Meadow. Jonquil will…"

No job for Primrose herself, I'll bet, thought Laurel. As Primrose read on, Laurel tilted her head back and gazed at the leafy branches overhead. Her mind wandered to the long-ago fairies who had woven the branches of young trees together. The branches had stayed that way as the trees grew skyward. Now they formed a green canopy over the Ancient Clearing. The sun trickled through, sprinkling drops of light on the heads of the listening fairies.

The sound of her own name caught her attention. "And Laurel's job is to water the gardens."

Surprised, Laurel just nodded. She'd expected Primrose to give her a much worse task. Something boring like dusting pinecones or scrubbing rocks. Carrying water would almost be fun. At least she'd be able to move around.

Primrose instructed everyone to report back for evening jobs. Then the meeting broke up.

All afternoon, the young woodfairies worked away at

their tasks. Laurel made trip after trip to the stream to fill her bucket with water. Then she carried it back to the newly planted garden.

Her slippers soon grew soggy from water that insisted on splashing out of the bucket. The dirt on them then turned to mud.

At least I've managed to keep my dress pretty clean, thought Laurel with satisfaction.

She was dumping water on the last section of garden when something caught her eye. There was a strange shimmering at the edge of the garden.

It couldn't be sunlight, Laurel realized. That part of the garden was now shaded. Besides, there was a mysterious glow to the light. Like a star fallen from the night sky.

"How strange," Laurel said aloud. "I wonder what it is?"

She put down her bucket and threaded her way through the rows of seedlings. Then as Laurel came close, the shape suddenly darted off to the left.

Startled, Laurel lost her footing. As she landed on the muddy ground, the light faded and vanished. At the same time, Laurel heard something. It was halfway between a giggle and the silvery sound of water rushing over rocks.

For a moment, Laurel thought another woodfairy had seen her fall. Maybe Primrose. But Primrose wasn't a giggler. Besides, there was no sign of Primrose—or of any other woodfairy. As for the light…Well, it was definitely gone.

I'm imagining things, thought Laurel.

She picked herself up and peered at the back of her dress. From what she could see, her skirt was caked with mud.

"Wonderful!" sighed Laurel. "I'd better get changed or I really will hear some giggles!"

She picked up her bucket and hurried home. Her treehouse near Thunder Falls was only a short walk from the garden. Too close to bother flying.

At the base of the giant oak where she'd built her home, Laurel spotted something. "What's that?" she murmured.

Bending over, she picked up a lone slipper. "I wonder how one of my slippers ended up here?" she asked. "And how did it get so dirty?"

Then she shrugged. Sometimes it was hard to remember where she put things. Or how they got dirty.

Slipper in hand, she flew to her porch and went inside. There she shed her muddy clothing. She tossed everything in the corner—including the mystery slipper. Then she put on a clean dress and shoes and ran a comb through her tangled curls.

"That's better!" she said as she checked her image in the mirror. She made her way to the ground and hurried toward the clearing.

Along the way, Laurel thought about the day's events. Even though the young fairies were on their own, things had gone fairly well. And Laurel had to admit that Primrose deserved some of the credit for that. Maybe Laurel would even tell her so.

Unless, of course, the muddy slipper was a trick on Primrose's part.

Laurel was still considering that when she reached the clearing. Ivy was watching for her, a worried look on her usually calm face.

"What's the matter?" Laurel asked her friend. Wordlessly, Ivy motioned toward the scene before them. A crowd of young woodfairies was gathered around a tree. A woven rug had been hung there to dry after washing. Now several wood-fairies were pointing at the rug and shaking their heads.

Before Ivy could answer, Primrose stepped out of the crowd. With her wings quivering, she marched over until she stood nose to nose with Laurel. An awful silence fell over the clearing.

"This isn't funny, Laurel," she snapped. "Not funny at all."

Mysterious Mischief

aurel sighed. "All right, Primrose. I give up. What's not funny?"

"You know what I'm talking about!" replied Primrose. She pointed an accusing finger at the rug. "That!"

"I know what it is," said Laurel. "It's the rug that goes on Mistress Marigold's porch. Why does it have you all so upset?"

But as Laurel moved closer, she saw what was wrong. Very muddy feet had stomped right across the music teacher's rug. And the footprints had obviously been made by the soles of fairy slippers.

Laurel shook her head and turned to look at the other woodfairies.

At once Primrose attacked. "I'm sure you think it's terribly funny, Laurel. But we don't have time for nonsense."

"I didn't do it!" Laurel protested. "And I think it's messy—not funny."

"Ha!" snorted Primrose.

A sudden suspicion occurred to Laurel. "Maybe you did it," she accused Primrose. "I found one of my slippers by my treehouse. It was covered with mud too."

"Me! *You* might enjoy playing silly little tricks like this. I don't!" snapped Primrose.

She glared at the muddy footprints and then swung back

11

to Laurel. "Well, we don't have any more time to waste arguing. We have to get busy with the evening chores. Which will take a little longer tonight, thanks to someone."

Laurel bit back her reply. No matter what she said, Primrose would think she was guilty.

Primrose stalked back to the center of the clearing. Rolling out her chore list, she read assignments in a frosty voice.

It came as no surprise that Laurel's chore was to wash the rug. Laurel didn't think it was fair. Still, someone had to clean up the mess before Mistress Marigold returned. And Laurel *did* have more experience with removing mud than most woodfairies.

However, Laurel soon found that cleaning the rug wasn't easy. The mud was ground in, for one thing. Besides that, she kept missing spots.

Luckily Ivy finished her chore early and came to help. Laurel was grateful, but upset that her friend didn't say much.

Finally Laurel put down her bar of soap and stared at Ivy. "It wasn't me," she said. "I think Primrose did it."

Ivy paused and frowned. "It doesn't seem like something Primrose would do. In fact, I don't know who would bother with such mischief right now."

"Neither do I," said Laurel. She sighed and went back to her scrubbing.

〜

The next day, Laurel woke up determined to prove herself. She'd be the hardest-working fairy in all of the Dappled Woods.

Laurel hurried through her morning job. Again she was in charge of watering the gardens. This time she managed to do it without getting muddy. And she didn't allow anything to interrupt her.

Laurel quickly finished her afternoon chores too. She was supposed to sweep the porches of the older fairies' cabins. Between sneezes, a few fairies complained about all the dust she stirred up. Still, the porches had never been so clean.

It was a very self-satisfied Laurel who headed home to her treehouse. By the time she arrived, the evening light was fading. So it took a minute before she realized what she was seeing.

Something was dangling overhead, just out of reach.

It was her traveling bag. And the bag was hanging from her favorite sash. Which was tied to her second-best hair ribbon. Which was tied to one of her stockings. And so on, all the way up to the porch railing of her treehouse.

"What in the world?"

At the sound of Laurel's voice, the bag began to wiggle. Then in a clear but weak voice, it squeaked, "Help!"

At once Laurel went into action. She reached up and grabbed the bag in one hand. Then she flew up to her porch. Ribbons and sashes—half her wardrobe, it seemed—trailed along behind.

Quickly Laurel loosened the drawstring and opened the bag. Chitters shot from his prison like an arrow from a bow. He was followed by an outraged Mistletoe.

"What were you two doing in there?"

asked Laurel.

"It was horrible! Terrifying! Unspeakable!" cried Chitters.

Laurel turned to Mistletoe. Maybe she could get an answer from the wise little mouse.

"I'm not sure what happened, Laurel," Mistletoe said. "We were just sitting on the ground, waiting for you to come home. Suddenly someone threw your bag over our heads. The next thing we knew, we were swinging in the air."

"Did you see anyone? Or hear anything?"

"Nothing! Not at all! Absolutely not!" replied Chitters.

"We saw a strange shadow," Mistletoe gently corrected him. "And I thought I heard a giggle. I couldn't be sure, though. Chitters was eating a nut, and you know how noisy that can be."

"It was Primrose!" cried Laurel. "I know it was!"

She began to pace back and forth across the porch. "She's jealous, that's all. I've told her over and over again that she could talk to animals too. *If* she'd only listen. But no, she can't listen."

"Laurel—" Mistletoe tried to interrupt.

"She just has to talk and talk all the time. Giving orders. Bossing people around."

"Laurel—"

"She never lets anybody else get in a word. Still, I can't believe she'd do something this mean. This rotten. This—"

"Laurel!" A sharp tug on Laurel's headwreath got her attention. "Listen!" said Mistletoe, who had jumped onto the fairy's shoulder. "I don't think it was Primrose."

"Well, I do!" declared Laurel. "You don't know how mad she is at me. It was Primrose. I'm sure of it. And I'm not putting up with any more. I'm going to give her a piece of my mind!"

With that, she stepped off the porch and fluttered to the ground. Then, wings trembling with anger, she stalked down the path toward Primrose's cabin. The two animals darted along at her heels.

The light was nearly gone by the time Laurel reached the cabin. However, she could see Primrose. The fairy was sitting on her front step, working by lantern light. Several other woodfairies were standing nearby, including Ivy.

"All right, Primrose! I've had enough!" shouted Laurel.

Everyone stared at her in surprise. Even for Laurel, shouting was unusual.

Primrose didn't say a word. Instead she slowly rose to her feet. Laurel noted that the woodfairy was holding a journal in her hand.

To everyone's horror, Primrose hurled the book directly at Laurel.

Laurel ducked and the journal landed harmlessly behind her. Primrose glared. Then she whirled about and headed into her cabin, slamming the door.

"Hey!" called Laurel. "*I'm* the one who's supposed to be mad!"

There was no response from the cabin. Laurel glanced at the other woodfairies. Some were studying her as if she were a stranger. Even Ivy was giving her an odd look.

"Ivy, what's going on?" she asked.

"Someone ruined Primrose's new journal," replied Ivy. "The one she's been working on for weeks."

Laurel bent over and picked up the journal. She remembered seeing it before. Primrose had spent hours decorating the cover with leaf and flower shapes. It had been perfect, of course.

Had been. Now it was a soggy mess. Mud and dirt streaked the covers and several pages were torn.

"Surely you don't think that I—" said Laurel. She broke off, unable to continue.

"I found it," Violet piped up.

"Where?" asked Laurel, her heart sinking.

"In the pond below the falls," answered Violet. "Right near your treehouse."

CHAPTER THREE

No Laughing Matter

t took Laurel a moment to grasp what Violet had said. Then she marched to the porch and rapped on Primrose's door.

Silence greeted her. So Laurel knocked again—louder this time.

Finally, at her third try, the door popped open. Primrose stood there, her face an unhealthy red. "You might as well come in and ruin everything I own. Get it all over with."

"Come on, Primrose!" protested Laurel.

Primrose shook her head and pointed at her ruined journal. "This was really nasty, Laurel!"

Violet stepped forward. "Primrose is right. You're being mean now."

"I am not!" cried Laurel. "I never even touched Primrose's journal!"

"Well, you were mean to me this morning!" said another fairy. "When I walked under your treehouse, you shot at me!"

"I what?" asked Laurel.

"You shot at me!" insisted the fairy. She held up a flute. "Then you dropped this on my head. You used Mistress Marigold's flute as a peashooter."

Hot tears pricked against Laurel's eyelids. How could anyone believe she'd do such things? Did they honestly think she was that unkind?

She opened her mouth to speak. However, she was afraid that if she said anything, she'd start to cry. So she just laid Primrose's wet journal on the step. Then, still silent, she headed back down the path. She hadn't gone far before she started to run. All she could think about was getting back to her treehouse.

"Laurel!" called Ivy.

But Laurel didn't answer.

For once the early morning sunlight didn't cheer Laurel. She'd tossed and turned all night. Dirty rugs, soggy journals, and musical peashooters had filled her mind.

Another uncomfortable thought had made its way in there too. She couldn't understand how anyone could blame her for such mean tricks.

Yet she'd been just as quick to blame Primrose.

In her heart, Laurel knew that Primrose would never try to frighten Mistletoe and Chitters. She might make fun of Laurel for talking to animals. However, like all woodfairies, Primrose loved the creatures of the forest.

Laurel pushed aside the filmy canopy that hung over her bed and sat up.

"I'm not the one playing all these tricks," she sighed.

"And I suppose it's probably not Primrose either. So just who *is* responsible?"

She sat there thinking for a bit. Finally she stood up. "I'm going to talk to Primrose. That is, if she'll let me. We need to figure out what's going on."

Quickly Laurel dressed. She grabbed a handful of berries for breakfast and headed for the clearing. Primrose would be there, she was sure.

Laurel's confidence faded as soon as she neared the Ancient Clearing. Something was wrong, she could tell. A large group of woodfairies was gathered just outside the Eldest's cabin, close to the clearing. In their midst was Primrose. Just beyond her lay the Eldest's pride and joy: her flower garden. It was one of the prettiest sights in the Dappled Woods, especially in spring.

At least it had been yesterday. Today the garden was a mess of shredded leaves and muddy soil. Blossoms lay scattered across the porch.

"Really, Laurel!" exclaimed one woodfairy. "How could you do such a thing?"

"I-I-I…," Laurel stammered, and then choked on her own words.

At last Primrose lifted her eyes from the ruined garden. Then she quietly announced, "I don't think it was Laurel who did this."

Laurel stared at the other fairy in surprise. She certainly hadn't expected Primrose to defend her.

"Why not?" asked Violet. "Laurel's the one who's been playing tricks on everyone."

Primrose sighed. "I'm not saying she didn't play a lot of tricks. I'm just saying she wasn't responsible for this. Laurel would never do such a thing to the Eldest. Never."

For a moment. Laurel and Primrose studied each other. At last Laurel said, "No, I wouldn't. In fact, I haven't done any of these tricks. At least, not the mean ones. And I came to tell you that I'm sorry for blaming you about Chitters and Mistletoe."

"What?" gasped Primrose.

Laurel went on to describe what had happened to the two animals. She ended by explaining how she'd finally realized that Primrose would never think of such a thing.

"Well! I should hope not!" snapped Primrose. Then she shrugged. "I guess I was pretty quick to blame you too. Even though Ivy kept telling me I was wrong."

She went on. "After all, Laurel, you have done some silly things."

"Like hanging people's paintings upside down?" Laurel asked.

"All right. Maybe I did that," Primrose admitted.

"And maybe I hid your paintbrush. But I don't play mean, nasty tricks. Do I?"

After a moment, Primrose shook her head. Most of the other woodfairies shook their heads as well.

"Well, if neither one of us is responsible for what's going on, who is?" demanded Laurel. "And what are we going to do about it?"

"You're asking me?" said Primrose.

"Yes," replied Laurel. "After all, you're kind of in charge, aren't you?"

"Well...I guess."

A gentle voice spoke up. "Why don't you both talk about it?" suggested Ivy. "Meanwhile, the rest of us will try to repair some of the damage. I have an idea for how we might fix Primrose's journal."

"I know where we can dig up some flowers," offered Violet. "So we can replant the Eldest's garden."

Laurel and Primrose eyed one another doubtfully. Then both nodded.

"Come on," said Primrose. "We'll go talk in my cabin."

The other woodfairies scattered, all eager to get things back to normal. Laurel and Primrose walked along in silence.

As Laurel entered Primrose's cabin, she noted that nothing was out of place. As usual. Three hammock chairs that Primrose had woven hung from the ceiling—in a straight row. Cushions were fluffed and the tablecloth hung evenly. There wasn't a dirty dish or sash in sight.

Laurel sank into one of the hammocks and sighed. "Do you have any idea what's going on?"

"No," answered Primrose. "I even checked the Chronicles after I noticed the Eldest's garden. I wanted to see if anything like this had happened before."

The Chronicles contained the entire written history of the fairies. When anything of note occurred, that's where it was recorded.

"And?" asked Laurel.

"Nothing," admitted Primrose.

"Maybe we should go and tell the Eldest what's been happening," suggested Laurel.

"Absolutely not!" said Primrose in her bossiest tone. "We

have to figure this out for ourselves. After all, we're not going to be the youngest fairies much longer. We need to learn how to handle problems on our own."

"You may be right," agreed Laurel. "But I'm not sure how to handle this one. Are you?"

Excited shouts drowned out the question. Laurel and Primrose jumped to their feet and ran outside. There they saw Jonquil and Daffodil running full speed toward the cabin. Both were gasping for air—and sobbing.

"Primrose! Laurel!" cried Jonquil.

"It's awful!" wailed Daffodil.

Fear tightened Laurel's chest. "What's wrong?" she asked.

"We went to Moonlight Meadow," said Daffodil. "And they're all gone!"

"What's gone?" asked Primrose.

"The fairy dandelions! There's not a trace of them left!"

CHAPTER FOUR

Disaster Strikes!

hat can't be!" exclaimed Laurel. "The dandelions can't be gone."

"They are," replied Jonquil, brushing away tears. "Every last one of them."

"I need to see for myself," said Laurel in a dull voice. She pushed past Primrose, who seemed frozen in place.

Laurel felt frozen herself, though her legs were moving. Now she saw other woodfairies heading their way, most with tears on their cheeks.

Quickly the group made its way to the meadow. Normally there was no more beautiful, joyous spot in the Dappled Woods. Sunlight played on the trees that gracefully ringed the meadow. A gentle brook sang softly, accompanied by the birds. And a warm breeze playfully teased the long grass.

But where fairy dandelions had grown yesterday, only holes could be seen. Not a flower head, stem, or leaf remained.

"Who could have done this?" Primrose asked.

Her question broke the spell of silence that had gripped the fairies. High, frightened voices began to ask questions.

"Where are our dandelions?"

"What are we going to do now?"

"What will we tell the Eldest and the mistresses?"

Laurel waited for Primrose to say something. She'd have a

suggestion—she *always* had a suggestion. Laurel might not agree with all of Primrose's ideas. Still, right now she'd be grateful just to hear the other fairy's sure voice.

To her surprise, Laurel spotted Primrose sitting quietly, head in hands.

"Primrose!" Laurel called. "What should we do?"

Primrose slowly lifted a tear-stained face. "Do? How should I know?"

Laurel had been frightened before. Now she was terrified. Primrose admitting that she didn't know something?

Primrose lowered her head and began to trace shapes in the dirt with one finger. That worried Laurel too. It was so unlike neat-and-tidy Primrose.

"I think it's all connected," said Laurel.

Primrose didn't respond. It was Daffodil who asked, "What do you mean?"

"The nasty tricks someone's been playing on us," replied Laurel. "I think the same person is responsible for all of that— and for this."

A murmur ran through the crowd of fairies. Primrose scrubbed at her tears with one hand, unaware of how grubby her fingers were.

"Does that make sense, Primrose?" asked Laurel. She had to get Primrose to start thinking.

Primrose just shook her head.

"Maybe Laurel's right," said Violet. She looked at Laurel hopefully. "How can we fix this?"

Laurel's face fell. Voice faltering, she said, "I don't think we can. And that means…"

Another fairy finished what Laurel couldn't. "The new woodfairies won't be born."

After that, no one said anything. The young fairies stared out at the ruined meadow, lost in black thoughts.

At last Ivy spoke. "We'd better get the Eldest."

"No!" snapped Primrose.

Everyone gazed at her in surprise.

"Primrose—" began Laurel.

"We're supposed to be responsible for the Dappled Woods right now!" exclaimed Primrose. Her voice was thick with unshed tears. "We can't bother the Eldest and the mistresses. Not when they're busy getting ready for the new fairies."

Then she stopped, remembering that without the dandelions, there'd be no new fairies.

"I should have asked someone to guard the meadow," moaned Primrose. "This is all my fault."

"It's no more your fault than anyone else's," replied Laurel, surprising herself. But it was true.

"I think Ivy was right," Laurel continued. "We have to tell the Eldest. Before we do that, though, let's think things through. Did anyone notice anything unusual lately? Besides the stupid tricks, I mean."

"Like what?" asked Daffodil.

"Strange sounds. Lights and shadows. Anything at all."

At first no one answered. Then Ivy said, "It felt like someone was watching me while I was picking flowers. I told myself it was just my imagination."

Jonquil nodded. "I know what you mean. I had the same feeling. And yesterday I left some nuts in a basket by my door. When I came home, there were only shells there."

Laurel spoke next, telling about the giggles and lights in the garden. Then other fairies added their own observations. They remembered odd rustling noises. Missing items. Whispers in the underbrush. Shadows at cabin windows.

Still, no one had actually seen any prowlers in the Dappled Woods.

Finally the fairies fell silent. Laurel looked at Primrose expectantly. Primrose returned her gaze.

In the end, Primrose nodded. "I'll fetch the Eldest and the others."

"I'll come too," offered Laurel.

"We'll wait for you here," said Ivy.

Laurel and Primrose hurried off toward the quiet grove at the edge of the woods. Once there, they hesitated. Then with lowered heads, they entered the grove.

As they'd expected, the mistresses were gathered around the Eldest. All seemed surprised to see the two young wood-fairies. Several appeared annoyed at the interruption.

But the Eldest's voice was all gentle concern. "What's wrong?" she asked. "Is someone hurt?"

"No," said Primrose. "That is, we're all fine. It's just—"

"It's the fairy dandelions," broke in Laurel. She took a deep breath before continuing. "They're gone!"

The Eldest turned pale. Slowly she sat down. The journal in her hands fell unnoticed to the ground.

After a stunned silence, the older fairies gathered around Laurel and Primrose. They peppered them with worried questions.

At last the Eldest held up a hand for silence. "We must go to the meadow and see what we can find out," she said.

In short order, the older woodfairies joined the others at

the meadow. They too were struck dumb by the awful scene.

One at a time, Laurel and Primrose told them all that had been going on. They even admitted the tricks they'd played on one another. And Laurel explained her idea that everything was connected.

"You may be right, Laurel," said the Eldest. "Or it could also have been an animal who dug up the dandelions. Perhaps they were dragged into the bushes. Let's spread out and search. If we find some, we can replant them and hope for the best."

"Will that work?" asked Mistress Marigold.

"I don't know," admitted the Eldest. "The woodfairies have never had to face this problem before."

"We might never have to again," Mistress Gooseberry sourly noted. "No fairy dandelions means no seeds. That means no dandelions in the future. And we all know what that means."

"Let's not give up hope yet," replied the Eldest.

Shaking her head gloomily, Mistress Gooseberry went off to search. So did the others.

But it proved useless. There wasn't a sign of the huge dandelions anywhere near the meadow.

It was a solemn group that gathered in the Ancient Clearing later. The Eldest cleared her throat. "It is clear that our dandelions aren't anywhere near here. We shall have to broaden our search if we hope to find them."

"If they *can* be found," muttered Mistress Gooseberry.

The Eldest ignored the comment. "It may turn out that whoever—or whatever—stole the dandelions took them out of the Dappled Woods."

"You mean into the Great Forest?" asked Daffodil fearfully.

The thought of going into the forest, even to find their

28

precious dandelions, alarmed her. As it did all the woodfairies. Except Laurel, of course. So no one was surprised when the Eldest's eyes fastened on her.

"I'll go, Eldest," offered Laurel.

"I thought you might say that," smiled the old fairy. "However, you should have some help. It's dangerous in the Great Forest. I don't want you out there alone."

"I'll send Mistletoe and Chitters to fetch Foxglove," Laurel assured her. "He'll come with me."

The Eldest nodded. "Good. We all admire Foxglove's skills in the forest. I'm sure you'll be safe with him."

After that, the meeting broke up. Laurel sent Mistletoe and Chitters on their way to Old Warren with a message for Foxglove. Then she went home to get ready for the trip.

With her traveling bag packed, Laurel had nothing to do but wait. It would be evening before Foxglove arrived. And a party of fairies had left to search the farthest corners of the Dappled Woods—without her.

The longer Laurel waited, the darker her thoughts grew. What if she and Foxglove found the dandelions too late?

What if they couldn't find them at all?

Or what if the trolls had stolen the fairy dandelions?

She gulped at that last thought. The horrible creatures had captured Laurel and Foxglove once before. That time they'd managed to escape. Would they be so lucky a second time?

Laurel shook off her fears and stood up. Well, there were still chores to be done. Despite everything that had happened.

She was just returning from watering the garden when Ivy raced up.

"Foxglove's here," Ivy told her friend.

Laurel followed Ivy to the clearing. It was crowded with

fairies, all gathered around the pixie. All trying to tell him at once what had happened.

When he saw Laurel, Foxglove broke free. "Laurel! I heard about the dandelions. What does it mean? If someone took them, did they take the new fairies too?"

"No," replied Laurel. "Remember, I told you that the fairies aren't actually inside the dandelions yet. But without the dandelions, they'll never appear."

Foxglove frowned. "Tell me what I can do to help."

"You can come with me into the Great Forest," said Laurel. "To see if we can track down the thief and get the dandelions back."

"First let me check the meadow," said Foxglove. "I might find a clue or two."

The Eldest led the way to the meadow. There Foxglove inspected the holes that had been left behind. Then he set off, walking along the edges of the field.

Halfway down the third side, the pixie came to a halt. Laurel saw a thoughtful look come over his face. He examined a thorny bush and plucked something from a branch.

With that, his inspection seemed to be finished. Foxglove marched back across the field to the waiting fairies.

"Well, I know who your tricksters are," he said with a frown. "And it's not good news."

CHAPTER FIVE

An Unexpected Volunteer

rolls?" asked Laurel in a horrified whisper. "Was it trolls?"

"No," said Foxglove. "You have sprites. Or rather, you *had* sprites. I'm sure they're long gone."

"Sprites?" asked Mistress Marigold. "What are sprites?"

"Not what," replied Foxglove. "Who."

"I thought you'd told me about all the creatures of the Great Forest, Foxglove," remarked Laurel. "But you've never mentioned sprites. Where do they live? Can you take me there?"

Foxglove frowned. "That's the bad news part, I'm afraid." He looked at the sea of frightened faces. "Let me explain."

Foxglove sat down on a nearby stump. "I never mentioned sprites before because I didn't think they came around here anymore. I haven't heard anyone talk of sprites since I was a tiny pixie."

"How can you be so sure they're here now?" demanded Mistress Gooseberry.

"This is how," replied Foxglove. He opened his hand.

The fairies moved closer to see what Foxglove was holding.

"A cobweb?" said Ivy.

"Milkweed?" asked Laurel.

"It's a ringlet of hair," replied Foxglove. "I found it on a bush. There's only one creature with curls like this. A sprite."

31

As Laurel watched, the ringlet began to shimmer with a delicate light. The light faded, then brightened again.

"I think that's what I saw in the garden," she decided. "Though I didn't see a sprite attached to it. At least I don't think I did."

"No one sees a sprite unless it wants to be seen," Foxglove told her.

"What would sprites want with our dandelions?" asked the Eldest.

"And what about all the tricks that they played on us?" asked Laurel.

Foxglove quickly turned to her. "Tricks? What tricks?"

As soon as Laurel had filled him in, Foxglove nodded. "Makes sense. Sprites aren't evil like trolls. They don't try to hurt or capture other creatures. They don't care about gold or land or other treasures. But they're full of mischief. They love pranks and jokes."

He scratched his head. "I still don't understand. Sprites stay away from places as calm and peaceful as your woods."

Laurel and Primrose exchanged a guilty look. "Things haven't been as calm and peaceful as usual around here," Laurel said quietly.

"No, they haven't," admitted Primrose.

The Eldest looked from Laurel to Primrose before addressing Foxglove. "You still haven't told us why they'd take our dandelions, Foxglove."

"Maybe they were hungry," said the pixie.

"Hungry!" cried Laurel. "You mean they might have eaten our dandelions?" Outraged cries greeted her words.

"I don't know for sure," Foxglove said. "But I'm afraid it's a possibility. I've heard that dandelions are considered a treat by sprites. They'd probably never seen any so big before."

"So big that maybe they didn't eat them all," said Laurel. "They might have taken some home with them."

She appealed to her friend. "Let's go to wherever it is the sprites live, Foxglove. To see if any of the dandelions are left."

"I'm sorry, Laurel. We can't do that."

"Why not?" asked Laurel.

"Because they don't actually live anywhere. They just kind of wander from place to place."

"Then we'll follow their trail until we catch up to them," declared Laurel.

"Okay," said Foxglove. "We'll leave in the morning. There's no sense heading out now. We won't be able to track them in the dark."

Then the pixie addressed the other woodfairies. "I just don't want any of you to get your hopes too high," he said.

"I'm afraid that this is our *only* hope," said the Eldest.

For a moment, Foxglove and the old fairy locked eyes. A wordless message passed between them. Laurel knew that the Eldest was telling Foxglove that she trusted him. And that Foxglove was promising to do his best.

Suddenly a voice broke the silence. "You'll need help."

Foxglove and Laurel spun around to see who was speaking. There stood Primrose, hands on hips. The old determined expression was back.

She took a deep breath and then flatly stated, "I'm coming with you."

CHAPTER SIX

Tracking the Tricksters

or a moment, Laurel was too shocked to respond to Primrose. But only for a moment.

"No!" she declared loudly. "You can't come." She turned to appeal to the forest expert. "Tell her, Foxglove!"

However, the pixie was no help. He just shrugged.

Laurel frowned and continued. "It's dangerous out in the Great Forest, Primrose. Really dark and wild and strange. You wouldn't like it."

"Don't forget, I've been out there before," said Primrose angrily. She addressed Foxglove, "Have you forgotten?"

"Um, no. Of course I haven't," murmured Foxglove. He gave Laurel a helpless look.

Laurel knew that Primrose had a point. Primrose didn't like leaving her home any more than the other fairies did. Still, she had done it once. She'd gone with the rest of the wood-fairies to save the pixie village from a terrible fire.

"Laurel…," said Foxglove. He started to argue, then fell silent when he saw her face.

Laurel's lips tightened. But before she could reply, a quiet, firm voice spoke up. "Primrose should go."

"Eldest?" In surprise, Laurel whirled to face the older woodfairy. "Primrose doesn't…" Her words faded as she studied the Eldest's expression.

"There are reasons why both you and Primrose need to do this," replied the Eldest. Her dark eyes seemed to drill into Laurel.

Primrose stepped closer. "That's right, Laurel. I need to come with you because it's our...Because it's partly *my* fault that this happened," she said. "You heard what Foxglove told us about the sprites. They're attracted to places where there's a lot of noise and trouble. Well, there was a lot of noise and trouble here. I helped cause it."

Laurel glared at Primrose. And Primrose glared back. Meanwhile, Foxglove examined his feet thoughtfully.

Laurel was the first to lower her eyes. Primrose was right, of course. She *was* partly responsible—as was Laurel.

"Okay," Laurel said at last. "Come with us. But you can't complain about getting dirty. Or about being tired. And you can't be in charge of things like you always want to be. Not out in the Great Forest."

At that, Foxglove spoke up. "*I'll* be in charge," he announced. "Or we're not going."

The Eldest nodded. "Then it's settled," she said. She placed one hand on Laurel's shoulder and the other on Primrose's. Both young fairies studied her wise face.

"I know you may not be able to find the dandelions," the Eldest said. "I also know you'll both try your hardest."

Laurel's gaze went from the Eldest to the other fairies who stood nearby. She could still see a few teary eyes and more than a few grim faces. Yet all looked at her with hope.

"We will," she promised.

"You need to pack a traveling bag tonight," Foxglove told Primrose. "Bring some dry clothing, extra shoes, and food. We'll leave tomorrow—at first light."

Primrose nodded and dashed off toward her cabin.

While Primrose was gone, Foxglove talked to Chitters and Mistletoe. The animals had wanted to come along, but Foxglove had other plans for them. They were to help the fairies as they continued to search along the edges of the Dappled Woods.

Laurel left them there and headed home to her treehouse. She knew Foxglove would find a spot to sleep for the night, as he always did.

As she walked along, Laurel's mind was a jumble of thoughts. And most of them weren't generous. She didn't want Primrose to come. It wasn't just because Laurel knew the journey might be dangerous. It was also because she didn't want to share this part of her life. She was the only woodfairy who went adventuring with Foxglove. Though she sometimes complained about feeling different, this was one difference she liked. She didn't want it to change.

Yet Laurel realized that if the dandelions weren't found, everything would change. There'd be no new woodfairies—different or alike.

So if Primrose could help, that was all that mattered. They'd just have to work together, she decided. Somehow…

It was a shaky decision, but Laurel felt a bit better. She flew up to her treehouse and settled down for the night.

❧

The sky was barely light when Laurel set off for the Ancient Clearing the next morning. So she was surprised to see many of the fairies already gathered there.

Foxglove was in the clearing as well, talking to the Eldest.

When he saw Laurel, he bowed to the old fairy and moved toward Laurel.

"I'm ready," she said, holding up her traveling bag.

Foxglove nodded. Then hesitantly he said, "Laurel, you have to promise me something. You and Primrose have to try to get along."

Despite her decision to do just that, Laurel was stung. "Don't worry," she shot back. "*I* won't be your problem!"

Foxglove merely shook his head. They waited in silence until Primrose arrived.

The farewells were painful for everyone. So Laurel was relieved when Foxglove finally said, "It's time we were off."

With the pixie in the lead, the three adventurers began their journey. In no time at all, they had reached Moonlight Meadow.

Foxglove paused by the bushes. "We'll start here," he said. "This is where I found the ringlet of sprite hair."

He bent down and studied the ground carefully. Laurel did the same, though she had no idea what she was searching for. Primrose just watched.

"Aha!" said Foxglove at last. "A footprint!"

Laurel and Primrose stared at the grass.

"Where?" asked Primrose. "I don't see anything."

Laurel didn't either. But she wasn't about to admit it.

Foxglove pointed to a dent in the soft ground. It was so faint that Laurel would never have noticed it. She didn't understand how Foxglove had.

"This way," the pixie said. "I see another." He led them away from the meadow, into the trees along its border.

Within a half hour's time, they reached the edge of the fairy woods. Foxglove didn't pause. He just plunged into the dark, tangled forest. Laurel went next. Then, with one last longing look at the Dappled Woods, Primrose followed.

They walked on in silence. Foxglove kept his eyes on the ground, still searching for clues.

After a while, Laurel was able to spot signs of the sprites too. They were all faint and hard to see. The whisper of a footprint in the soft soil. A twig bent slightly toward the ground. Another curl of hair caught on a branch.

To Laurel's satisfaction, Primrose didn't notice any of these clues. Not until they were pointed out to her.

However, the signs were few and far between. And the only way to spot them was to go slowly.

"At this rate, we'll never find the dandelions before the full moon," sighed Laurel. "After that, it won't matter anymore."

"You have to face the fact that it might not matter anyway," said Foxglove. "Not if we discover that the sprites have eaten all your dandelions."

"Don't even suggest such a thing," said Laurel. "We have to—"

"Shhh!" ordered Foxglove. "I hear something."

A high-pitched scream from Primrose followed. Laurel spun about to see a shower of leaves pouring down over the fairy.

It was over in a matter of seconds. By then Primrose was buried up to her waist. She stood there shaking, hands over her eyes, wings tightly folded against her back.

"Oh, for goodness' sake, Primrose!" scolded Laurel. "It's only leaves. There's no need to scream like that."

Primrose opened one eye. Then the other. Seeing it truly was safe, she fought her way out of the pile.

"Well, you'd scream too if something suddenly fell on

you!" she snapped.

"Those leaves didn't just suddenly fall," said Foxglove. "Someone dumped them on you." He pointed into the branches overhead.

Sure enough, a vine net could be seen hanging there. As they watched, one last leaf tumbled out and slowly drifted downward.

"Who would do that?" asked Primrose.

"The sprites must have realized we're following them," said Foxglove. "So they've decided it's time for a little fun."

"It's time for a little sprite-catching," said Laurel firmly. "That's what I'd call fun."

"It may be harder than you think," commented Foxglove quietly.

On they went, searching for the sprites' trail. They moved even more slowly now. It was hard to study the ground while also watching for things falling from above. Primrose followed so closely, she almost stepped on Laurel several times. This did nothing to calm Laurel's nervousness.

Both woodfairies were darting glances overheard when Foxglove came to a halt. They immediately stopped too.

"What's the matter?" cried Primrose.

"Are you okay?" asked Laurel.

Foxglove was batting something away from his face. As he twisted around, they could see long strands wrapped around his body.

An angry "Ummmph!" was all they got in reply.

"Hold still!" Laurel ordered. "I'll try to get this stuff off you." She grabbed her friend—and found her hands stuck to his tunic!

Wildly Laurel tried to pull free. But in thrashing about,

she only managed to get tangled herself. She ended up attached to Foxglove, back-to-back.

"Primrose, help us!" she shouted.

Primrose darted anxiously about. "How?"

"I don't know!" wailed Laurel. "Think of something!"

Primrose reached out to touch the strings that bound Foxglove and Laurel together. At once she pulled back. "Ugh!" she said. "It's sticky."

"Primrose!" Laurel barked.

The woodfairy waved her hands. "All right, all right. Just give me a minute."

She spun about, searching the forest for answers. Then with a cry of triumph, she snatched at a leafy bush. Quickly she plucked some green leaves. Using them to protect her hands, she pulled the threads away from Laurel and Foxglove.

At last Foxglove and Laurel stepped clear of the sticky trap. Foxglove cleaned his face with a leaf. Laurel wiped her hands on her skirt.

"What is this?" Primrose asked in disgust. She scrubbed at her own hands with fresh leaves.

"Cobwebs," said Foxglove. "With tree sap on them."

"Another sprite trick, I suppose," said Laurel. "I can't wait to get hold of—"

"I hear something!" interrupted Primrose.

The others heard it as well. A silvery laugh not far from where they stood. In fact, it seemed to come from the bushes right in front of them.

That was too much for Laurel. She charged straight at the sound.

Laurel didn't get far before something tripped her up. As she reached out to brace her fall, she felt something beneath her fingers. Then it was gone.

"I almost had one!" she cried. "I touched it!"

Foxglove helped Laurel to her feet. And once again they heard it. A giggle echoing through the trees. But the sound was farther away now.

Laurel thought she saw a glimmer of light in the distance. Then both the light and laughter faded.

A frustrated silence followed. At last Primrose spoke up, "I have an idea. I think we should—"

Laurel broke in. "Foxglove is in charge out here. He's the one who knows the Great Forest. And the sprites."

"Just a minute, Laurel," said Foxglove. "I'm not doing so well. I'd like to hear what Primrose has to say."

"Fine," huffed Laurel. "Go ahead and listen."

Primrose gave Laurel an angry glare before going on. "I think we should turn the tables on the sprites," she said.

"What do you mean?"

"They've been setting traps for us. Let's do the same to them."

"What good would that do?" Laurel grumbled.

"A lot," Primrose declared. "If we can catch one, we can ask it about the dandelions."

Laurel didn't want to admit it, but Primrose's idea made sense. Anyway, setting a trap seemed smarter than walking into another one.

"We'll try it," said Foxglove. "And I've got a plan for how to do it." He dropped his voice and the fairies moved closer. "We'll set a snare. If both of you will lend me your sashes."

Laurel and Primrose shrugged, then untied the sashes at their waists. As he knotted the pieces of fabric together, Foxglove explained. "I'll make a loop," he whispered. "Then

41

lay it on the forest floor. When the sprite comes close, I'll pull the loop tight. He'll be trapped!"

"But why would he come close?" asked Primrose.

"To get the bait," replied Foxglove. He suddenly got very busy tying the sashes together. "We need something special to put in our trap. Something the sprite will want badly enough to risk coming out in the open." He paused before adding, "And I don't have anything like that in my scavenging bag."

"You must have something in your bag," Laurel said to Primrose.

"You must have something in *yours*," returned Primrose.

Foxglove sighed and both the woodfairies blushed. Laurel reached for her bag first. She searched a bit before pulling out a shiny blue stone. It was a treasure she'd found while adventuring with Foxglove one time. She always carried it with her—for good luck.

"Will this work?" she asked.

The pixie nodded. He took the stone from her and set it inside the loop. With Laurel's help, he covered the fabric with leaves. Then the three hid in the bushes nearby. Foxglove held the loose end of the tied sashes in his hand.

It seemed like they waited for hours. Laurel nearly fell asleep as she stared at the stone winking in the sunlight.

At last she saw a glimmer of light. She poked Foxglove and he nodded.

There was another glimmer— closer this time.

Then they saw the sprite. As before, it seemed made of sunshine and shadow, not flesh and blood. As they watched, the

sparkling shape became more solid and took on form.

Laurel eagerly studied the curious creature. The sprite was smaller than a woodfairy. Even smaller than a pixie. Its skin was pale green—the color of water bubbling over mossy rocks. It was also clothed in green.

As for the sprite's hair…Laurel simply couldn't tell what shade it was. The creature's tight ringlets caught and reflected light like a waterfall.

She watched as the sprite's bright eyes darted back and forth. It was definitely curious, Laurel saw. The creature's long, graceful fingers twitched. It stood on tiptoe to peer more closely at the stone.

Finally the sprite could stand it no longer. It dashed forward and grabbed the blue stone.

"Got ya!" shouted Foxglove as he yanked the loop tight.

The startled sprite whirled about. Then it leapt into the air—and disappeared.

Foxglove and the two woodfairies stared out at nothing. The stone was gone. So was the sprite.

"I warned you they were hard to catch," sighed the pixie.

"Great idea, Primrose," said Laurel. "Trying to trap something like that."

"It *was* a great idea!" Primrose shot back.

"Just like all your plans," Laurel snorted.

"Come on, you two," Foxglove began. "We can't—"

He paused. There was a scuffling sound. Then a splash.

Even as the pixie stood up to investigate, a terrible scream filled the forest.

CHAPTER SEVEN

Catching a Culprit

omeone's in trouble!" cried Laurel.

She took off in the direction of the scream. Foxglove and Primrose ran along behind her.

Laurel's first thought was that the sprites had trapped some other poor creature. Probably one of their stupid tricks had gone seriously wrong.

She crashed through a thick growth of bushes. There she came to a sudden halt. Foxglove and Primrose skidded to a stop beside her.

Before them stretched a great dark swamp. Within its slimy waters, a mud-covered figure struggled wildly.

As they watched, the trapped figure sank to its neck in the ooze. Only its green, fear-filled eyes could be seen through the layer of mud that coated it.

"It's the sprite!" exclaimed Primrose. "We caught it this time!"

"Well, we're going to lose it if we don't get it out of that mud!" said Laurel. She shouted to the sprite. "Hold still!" At the sound of her voice, the creature thrashed even harder.

"Stop wiggling!" ordered Foxglove. "We'll help you! But if you keep moving, you'll sink even more."

The sprite stopped struggling. Though it still seemed fearful, there was now a touch of hope in its eyes.

"We can't go out there," said Foxglove quietly. "Or we'll sink too."

"Maybe I could fly over and pull him out," suggested Laurel.

"Not out of swamp mud," said the pixie. "That stuff is so thick that it'll take all three of us to get him out."

Foxglove studied the swamp for a moment. "Break leafy branches off the bushes," he ordered. "As many as you can."

Laurel snapped off a large branch and brought it to Foxglove. He immediately placed it flat on the surface of the swamp. Then, stepping carefully, he walked on the branch.

Primrose crept out and handed him another branch. Foxglove laid that one just beyond the first.

They continued on, each branch taking them one step farther. The mud sucked greedily at their feet. But the branches held.

Soon the path reached all the way to the sprite. By now the creature had sunk even deeper into the mud. Its breath came in ragged gasps. Yet since that first scream, it had remained silent.

Foxglove eyed the sprite. Then he studied the branch beneath him. It was steadily sinking into the ooze.

"These branches won't hold us all—and the sprite," he said. "The two of you will have to fly."

At once Laurel and Primrose rose into the air.

"Okay," said Foxglove. "Everyone grab hold of the sprite's robe. When I give the signal, pull him toward me."

Laurel and Primrose dipped lower to grab the sprite's robe. Foxglove got a handful too. Then he braced himself as well as he could on the branches.

"All right—now!" shouted the pixie.

He gave a mighty yank. Wings beating madly, the wood-fairies tugged as well.

For one long moment, nothing happened. Then Laurel and Primrose began to sink closer to the swamp. It was as if the muddy waters had gripped them too.

They beat their wings even faster. Finally, with a great sucking sound, the swamp loosed its hold on the sprite. The little creature pulled free of the mud and flopped onto the branches.

"Got him!" Foxglove crowed.

Laurel and Primrose flew overhead as Foxglove and the sprite crawled across the leafy pathway.

At last all four were on solid ground again. Foxglove, Laurel, and Primrose were splattered with mud. The sprite was covered from nose to toes.

Foxglove grabbed his water pouch. "Hold still," he ordered before dumping the contents on the sprite.

The bath startled the sprite back into life. It sputtered and spit mud from between its teeth. Then it shook its wet curls, spraying water all over the others.

Primrose gritted her teeth. "All right. Enough of your little tricks. I've got some questions for you." She closed in on the soggy sprite.

The creature gave a giggle and jumped to its feet. Then it darted toward the bushes.

Primrose moved to block the sprite's way. Laughing, the creature circled around her.

That sent Primrose into a rage. With a great leap, she tackled the sprite. Down they both went in a whirl of fury.

"You're hurting me!" cried the sprite in a light, shimmery voice.

"Then stop trying to get away!" gasped Primrose.

Foxglove moved toward the struggling pair. He grabbed hold of the sprite's collar and pulled it away from Primrose.

Meanwhile, Laurel helped Primrose to her feet. She could hardly believe her eyes. Primrose was covered in dust and dirt. One edge of her skirt was torn and her headwreath hung crooked.

"You miserable little—" growled Primrose.

"You mean, nasty—" howled the sprite.

"That's enough!" shouted Foxglove. He pushed the sprite into a sitting position on a nearby log. It slumped there, sneaking peeks at Primrose from under its long green eyelashes.

"Come on, Primrose," said Laurel. "We want to ask him questions, not yell at him."

"I'm not a him," sniffed the sprite. "I'm a her. And I don't like the way she talks to me."

"I don't care what you like," responded Primrose. She stood over the sprite, hands on her hips and a fierce frown on her face.

The sprite squeezed her eyes shut. Two great tears leaked out and trailed down her pale green cheeks.

The pitiful effect was ruined when she opened one eye. She was clearly checking to see if anyone had noticed her fine performance.

Laurel felt her own temper beginning to flare. She took a deep breath. Then as calmly as she could, she asked, "Did you take our dandelions?"

"Dandelions?" echoed the sprite. "What dandelions do you mean?"

"You know very well what she means!" yelled Primrose.

"The huge dandelions from our meadow."

"Hmmm," said the sprite. "Let me think." She crossed her legs and leaned an elbow on her knee. Then she thoughtfully tapped her chin.

With an impatient snort, Primrose dove at the sprite.

Laurel held her back. It was clear that they weren't going to get anything from the sprite this way. They had to change their approach.

Laurel plunked down on the log next to the sprite. "What's your name?" she asked in a friendly fashion.

The sprite brightened. "I'm Peapod," she said. "Who are you?"

"I'm Laurel. And my friends are Foxglove and Primrose."

"Grimrose is more like it," said the sprite. "But I like you." She smiled at Laurel.

"Why, you little—" began Primrose.

Laurel interrupted. "We really need some help, Peapod. From someone who knows a lot about the forest."

The little sprite seemed interested—and flattered. "I know a lot. What kind of help do you need?"

"We're searching for some dandelions. Very special dandelions. It's important that we find them."

"I'll help you search!" volunteered Peapod. "I want some more dandelions too."

"More dandelions!" cried Primrose. "See! She does know about our dandelions!"

"Your dandelions. My dandelions. What's the difference?" asked Peapod curiously. She tilted her curly head and grinned at Primrose.

"Where are they?" asked Laurel gently. "Can you show me where you put our dandelions?"

"Sure," Peapod replied. She jumped up and patted her stomach. "Right here."

"You ate them?" asked Laurel.

The sprite thought this over. "Not all of them," she finally replied.

Relief washed over Laurel. Now if she could just convince the sprite to give her the remaining dandelions.

"Where are the ones you didn't eat?" she asked. "Can you show me?"

"Nope!" replied Peapod. She did a twirl and fell at Laurel's feet.

"Why not?" asked Laurel when Peapod stood up again.

Peapod giggled. "Because my friends ate the rest of them."

CHAPTER EIGHT

A Debt Repaid

ilence greeted Peapod's announcement. The sprite cocked her head and observed the others curiously.

"What's the matter?" Peapod asked. "Isn't that what you do with dandelions? I thought you liked them too."

Primrose nearly choked. "Liked them?" she shouted. "You...you...you..." Words failed her. She sank to the ground and buried her face in her hands.

"What's the matter with her?" Peapod asked. Laurel just shook her head.

So Peapod appealed to Foxglove. "What's the matter with them?" she asked.

"You wouldn't understand," said the pixie. "Those dandelions were important to the woodfairies. Very important."

"Well, I didn't know that," Peapod protested. "We were hungry. And there they were. Each one big enough to feed three sprites. So we took them."

Her bottom lip began to tremble. "They were just dandelions, that's all. If they were so important, why don't you just find some more?"

Primrose raised her head, ready to respond. But Laurel signaled her to be silent. To her surprise, Primrose closed her mouth.

Laurel sighed. "It's hard to explain, Peapod. You see, those dandelions only grow in that meadow in the fairy woods. They're really rare and wonderful flowers."

"Dandelions?" asked Peapod. "Rare and wonderful?"

"Those dandelions are," said Laurel. "They don't bloom very often. And when they do, it means that new woodfairies are going to be born."

"Oh," murmured the sprite. "Well, I'm sorry. How were we to know?"

Her sparkling eyes grew thoughtful. "It seemed like your woods were full of fairies. I almost got caught a couple of times. Don't you have plenty of fairies for now? Can't you wait until next year for more?"

"It doesn't happen very often. Certainly not every year," explained Laurel. "Besides, even if it did, you ate all the dandelions. So there won't be any seeds to grow new ones."

"Oh," said Peapod again. "I didn't think about that."

Primrose exploded. "You and your friends don't think about much at all, do you?"

"We do too! We're very good thinkers!" Peapod angrily replied. She moved closer to Laurel and motioned to her. When Laurel lowered her head, Peapod whispered, "I don't like her."

Sometimes I don't either, thought Laurel. But Primrose is right about this.

"She's just upset," explained Laurel. "So am I. Still, I believe you, Peapod. I know you didn't understand what you were doing."

Laurel continued, as if talking to herself. "What I don't know is what we can do now."

Foxglove broke the silence that followed. "You may as

well take off," he told the sprite.

"Really?" asked Peapod. "You're letting me leave?" She cast worried eyes in Primrose's direction.

Primrose just shrugged. "There's no way to fix this. So go. I never want to see a sprite again."

Peapod made a great leap, turning around in the air before landing. Then she scampered into the bushes. A faint shimmer marked the spot where she disappeared. In seconds that too vanished.

"How can we tell the others?" moaned Laurel.

"I don't know, Laurel," answered Foxglove. "I just don't know."

Primrose stood up. "We've failed," she muttered. "Totally and completely. We may as well go home and admit it."

So they set off, retracing their steps through the forest. They hadn't gone far before Foxglove paused. "I hear something!" he said.

They all listened. In the distance, Laurel heard birds twittering and leaves rustling. Nothing unusual or threatening.

Then there was a soft giggle.

"Go away!" shouted Primrose. "Stop following us, you miserable sprite!"

A familiar curly head popped out of the bushes. "I'm not miserable!" Peapod said. "You are."

With that, Primrose melted into tears. "Of course I am!" she sobbed.

Seeing Primrose fall apart was too much for Laurel. Her own lips started to quiver.

Peapod crawled out from the sheltering bush. "Stop crying," she begged. "I hate crying!"

A single tear trickled down Laurel's cheek. Primrose went

on sobbing loudly.

Peapod sent a troubled look Foxglove's way. "Can't you make them stop?"

Foxglove merely shrugged.

"Please stop!" Peapod begged. She drew closer and gently touched Laurel's arm. "I won't follow you again! I just wanted to see what you were doing, that's all. But I'll go away if you want me to!"

Laurel took a deep breath. "I'm not upset because you followed us," she said. "I'm upset about the fairy dandelions."

"Oh," said Peapod. "Well, don't worry about them. I'll help you find some more."

"There aren't any more," Laurel said. She wiped her damp cheeks with the back of one hand.

"You don't know that for sure," insisted Peapod. "You're a woodfairy. You hardly ever leave the Dappled Woods."

"Well, *I'm* not a woodfairy," declared Foxglove. "And I've never seen dandelions like that anywhere else."

"That doesn't mean there aren't any," said Peapod. "I'll take you to my camp. We'll ask the other sprites. Maybe someone has seen dandelions like yours."

The three adventurers exchanged glances. Then Foxglove spoke. "What do we have to lose? I say we go with Peapod."

"I don't trust her," declared Primrose. "She's probably just trying to trick us again."

"I am not!" exclaimed Peapod.

Laurel got up, ignoring their quarreling. "Let's go," she said. "I'm willing to try anything."

Peapod nodded happily. Then with a wave of her hand, she led them forward.

It wasn't easy to follow her. Peapod darted under low

branches and over fallen logs. Like a beam of light, the sprite seemed to flow smoothly wherever she pleased. It looked as though her feet hardly touched the earth.

"I think she's trying to wear us out," gasped Primrose at one point.

"I don't know about that," said Foxglove. "I'll tell you one thing, though. I've never seen this part of the forest before. Maybe there *are* more dandelions like yours somewhere."

Laurel had her doubts. However, she didn't voice them. She was too out of breath to speak. And she was a bit frightened. Maybe it was foolish to follow Peapod. The forest was so dark and wild here. What if the sprite deserted them? What if a troll found them?

Suddenly Laurel realized that the forest was growing brighter. At first she thought they might be approaching a clearing. Then she saw flickering lights here and there. Like a swarm of fireflies, the lights danced through the forest.

All at once, Peapod stopped. "We're here!" she exclaimed.

"Here?" repeated Primrose. "Where?"

"This is our camp," explained Peapod.

The others gazed blankly at the trees and bushes that grew thickly around them. Gradually Laurel realized that they were surrounded by sprites. With their green skin and clothing, the creatures blended in perfectly. They seemed to be everywhere. Hanging upside down from branches. Clinging to tree trunks. Peering from underneath bushes.

"Come on out, everybody!" called Peapod. "I've brought company."

A ripple of giggles greeted her announcement. Yet for several moments, no one moved.

Finally one sprite crept forward from his hiding spot. He reached out, touched one of Laurel's wings, and dashed back to the bushes.

Another appeared at Primrose's side and grabbed for her traveling bag. "Hey!" the woodfairy protested. Alarmed, the sprite tumbled head over heels.

The giggles grew louder. Then suddenly the sprites seemed to take courage. Several stepped forward together.

"Why are they here?" asked a whispery voice.

"Yes, why?" seconded another sprite.

"They need our help," said Peapod. "They're looking for dandelions."

"Lots of those," said a sprite. "They're everywhere."

"Not just any dandelions," said Peapod. She launched into her story, explaining about the fairies' special dandelions.

"How silly," remarked a sprite when Peapod finished. She gave a laugh and tickled her neighbor.

"It's not silly!" protested Laurel. "It's—"

"Why should we help?" another voice cut in.

The crowd parted to allow an elderly sprite through. His face was wrinkled with years, and his short, tangled curls were grayish-green.

The old sprite slowly made his way to the visitors. Then he repeated his question. "Why should we help you? Did you welcome us when we visited your forest? Does anyone ever welcome us?"

"No!" several sprites called out in response.

"Never!" said another.

"They just try to get rid of us!"

Laurel raised her hands to beg for silence. "We didn't even realize you were there. And even if we had, what could you expect? You just march in and cause all kinds of trouble."

"We weren't doing any harm," protested a chubby sprite. "We were just having fun."

"It wasn't fun for us," replied Laurel. "You ruined our things. And made us get angry at one another."

The plump sprite shrugged, but said nothing.

However, the old sprite moved closer. "I remember you," he said, staring into Laurel's face. "I watched you for most of one day. You like mischief as much as any sprite does. In fact, you made me feel right at home."

He nodded toward Primrose. "Especially when you stuffed moss in that one's flute," he added.

Laurel blushed. But before she could reply, the elderly sprite pinned Primrose with his sharp eyes. "And you," he said. "You laughed when you hung that painting upside down. Reminded me of myself when I was a youngster."

He wagged his finger. "So don't talk to me as if you wood-fairies don't like to have fun. I know better. And I don't see any reason why we should help you." With that, the old sprite turned his back on them.

"But—" Laurel began.

Peapod interrupted. "Wait, Twig. They helped me."

It was as though another unexpected visitor had walked into their midst. All the sprites fell silent and still. Several youngsters who'd been hanging from branches climbed down and moved closer. Twig stared at Peapod.

The sprite studied her audience. "I fell into the Great

Ooze," she said in a low voice.

A chorus of ooohs followed. The reaction seemed to satisfy Peapod. She waved her arms in the air as she continued her tale.

"You know how many of us have been lost there," she said solemnly. "I was sure I was next. I struggled as hard as ten wildcats. Still, I couldn't get free. The mud kept pulling me deeper and deeper, swallowing me up. Finally it reached my chin. That's when I screamed."

Here Peapod gave an awful shriek. The sprites all shrieked in response. Then, hanging on every word, they listened as Peapod told the story of her rescue.

At last Peapod wound up. "So, you see, they did help me. That's why I promised that we'd try to do the same for them."

Laurel eyed the crowd of sprites. Could they help? Would they help?

However, the excitement of the story seemed already forgotten. One tiny sprite began to twirl her way through the crowd, stepping on toes in the process. The young climbers went back to their branches.

Laurel felt her eyes burn with angry tears. They'd come all this way for nothing. "It's hopeless," she muttered to Foxglove and Primrose. "Let's see if we can find our way home."

But as they prepared to leave, a voice boomed out.

"Wait!"

A sprite stepped out of the shadow of a tree. As Laurel studied him, she noted that he was taller than the others. He also seemed more serious and steady. As he moved to Laurel's side, most of the sprites settled down again to listen.

"This is Burdock," said Peapod proudly. "The bravest and strongest sprite of all."

Burdock nodded in greeting. Then he said, "I guess we should thank you for saving little Peapod. We'd miss her."

"There's no need to thank us," said Laurel softly. "I'm glad we could save her."

Burdock tugged his ear thoughtfully. "To tell the truth, we sprites aren't very good at repaying debts. We've got little to pay with," he admitted with a grin. "Though I think I may be able to help you."

Laurel felt her heart leap. "Help us? How?"

"Well, I've seen some dandelions like yours before," Burdock said.

"Are you sure?" Laurel asked, her voice shaking.

"They glowed in the same way. And they were huge," the sprite answered. "Besides, I tasted one of them. It was the same."

He turned to his fellow sprites. "That's why I knew how delicious they were," he told them. "Because I'd eaten one before."

"Do you remember where you saw them?" asked Laurel excitedly. "Can you take us there?"

"I remember. I never forget anything," Burdock said with a laugh. Then his smile clicked off, making him seem older. "I can tell you where to find them. But I won't take you."

"Why not?" Primrose demanded.

Burdock's pale green skin took on a gray tint. He peered around at the other sprites before answering. "Because I can't," he said softly. "Because I'm afraid."

"You are not!" argued Peapod. She turned to Laurel. "Burdock is never afraid!"

"Yes, I am," said the tall sprite. "When I need to be. I'm not ashamed to admit it."

Looking toward Laurel, Burdock added, "I'll tell you where the dandelions are. Then you'll be afraid too."

"Why?" asked Laurel.

"Because those dandelions grow at the edge of the Bogs of Bleak. Where the trolls live."

Back to the Bogs

rolls. Laurel shivered at the very word. Trolls hated anything good and kind—and tried to destroy it. There was nothing more evil in the Great Forest. She'd seen that herself the time she and Foxglove had been captured by the trolls.

"Are you sure?" Foxglove asked, his voice unsteady. It was obvious that he too was remembering their capture.

"I know where I was," said Burdock. "I know what I saw. That's all I can tell you."

"I don't believe you!" declared Primrose.

Everyone looked her way. Laurel noted that Primrose was pale. She'd heard Laurel's tales of the trolls before.

Burdock shrugged. "Believe me or not. I don't care." He began to move away, stopping only when Laurel laid a hand on his arm.

"I believe you, Burdock," she said. "But the Bogs of Bleak are huge. Please help us find the dandelions."

Burdock studied Laurel's face. Finally he lowered his eyes and drew nervous lines in the dirt with his toes.

"I know it's scary," Laurel added gently. "But can you at least take us part of the way?"

Still not meeting Laurel's eyes, Burdock shook his head. "No. I can't. I saw a troll once. Smelled it too. I'm not getting anywhere near those beasts ever again."

"None of us will," said Twig. The other sprites nodded in agreement.

"Well, could you draw us a map?" asked Foxglove.

Burdock stared at the pixie blankly. "A map?" he asked. "What's a map?"

"You've got to be—" Primrose began. She fell silent when she saw Laurel's frown.

"It's like a picture," Laurel explained. "A picture that tells you how to get somewhere. Here, I'll show you."

She picked up a stick and crouched down to draw in the dirt. First she made a big circle. "Pretend this is the Great Forest," she said. Drawing a smaller circle, she said, "Here's your camp. Right in the middle of the forest."

At the mention of their camp, the other sprites crowded close. They watched as Laurel added to the map. She drew the trail she and her friends had taken. She showed where the pixie village and the Dappled Woods were located.

Finally, at the edge of her map, she scratched a wiggly line. "Here's the river," she said. "The trolls live on the other side."

Laurel turned to Burdock, who was sitting next to her. "Does this help? Can you point to the spot where you saw the dandelions?"

Burdock had been carefully reviewing the drawing. Now he snatched the stick from Laurel's hand. "That's not a map," he declared. "I'll show you a map."

Laurel fought back a sharp response. A minute ago, Burdock hadn't even known what a map was. Now he thought he was an expert.

Burdock drew a short line from the sprites' camp and added a circle. "This is where Rhubarb found his favorite rock," he commented.

"From there I went toward Sky Falls," he explained. He addressed the other sprites. "You all remember. The one we slid down last spring. After Skunkweed tumbled over."

As his friends nodded, Burdock drew a waterfall. Then inch by inch, he continued. Slowly his line crawled across the dirt as he described each step of his trip.

Laurel wanted to scream with impatience. But she'd seen enough of the sprites to know they wouldn't be rushed.

So she just waited, holding her breath—and hoping. The trolls feared rushing water more than anything. Actually, it was one of the *only* things they feared. Maybe the dandelions grew on this side of the river. If so, it might be possible to dig them up in safety. Even if they were close to the Bogs of Bleak.

"I got to the river," Burdock was saying at last. "There were lots of fish there." He sketched a fish near the lines that stood for the river.

"Dandelions too," he said. The sprite added a flower—on the trolls' side of the river.

"Are you sure that's where you saw them?" asked Foxglove.

"Yep," said Burdock. He dropped the stick, stood up, and stretched his arms.

"How did you get across the river?" asked Primrose.

Burdock yawned. "I rode across on a log. Grabbed a dandelion. Ate it. Then…"

"Then…," prompted Laurel when the sprite hesitated.

The grayish tint returned to Burdock's skin. "I smelled a troll. So I got out of there."

Laurel rose to her feet and looked at her pixie friend. "I don't expect you to go near the trolls again, Foxglove. Anyway, this is a woodfairy problem. I'll go alone."

Before Foxglove could say a word, Primrose broke in. "No, you won't. You're not the only woodfairy here. I'm coming too."

Laurel turned to tell Primrose what she thought about *that* idea. But one look into the other fairy's determined eyes changed her mind. That and the realization that she would be glad for any help she could get. "Thank you," she said at last.

"And you're not leaving me out of this," declared Foxglove. "You're my friend." He nodded toward Primrose and corrected himself. "My friends, I mean. So if you have a problem, so do I."

Laurel smiled at the pixie. Then she gave her attention to Burdock. "Thank you for helping us this much," she said. Burdock grinned and gave a sweeping bow.

The three friends took their leave of the sprites. A few farewells rang out—along with Peapod's shout of "Good luck!" However, in moments, most of the sprites seemed to have already forgotten they'd had visitors.

As they headed back into the gloom, Laurel voiced her concerns. "This could be a wild goose chase."

"I told you I didn't believe Burdock," agreed Primrose.

"I don't mean that," said Laurel. "I'll admit that I'm not sure his map was right. Still, I think he told the truth. It's just that I can't believe the dandelions Burdock saw are like ours. How could anything that good come from the trolls' bog?"

"Something else bothers me," admitted Foxglove. "Why

wouldn't the trolls have trampled those dandelions into the ground long ago? They hate things that are beautiful. Except for treasure."

Laurel shook her head. "Even if we do find the dandelions, I'm not sure our problems are solved. Let's say we dig them up and replant them in the Dappled Woods. Will fairies appear? Or does it only happen if the dandelions first take root in the fairy meadow?"

"There's no way we can know that," said Primrose.

"Well, I guess the first thing is simply to find them," sighed Laurel. "If we make it," she said with a shiver. "We have a long way to go, and the forest will only get wilder."

At that, Primrose inched closer to the others. Laurel gave the other woodfairy a smile. Someday I'll tell her how brave I think she is, thought Laurel.

For another hour, the three threaded their way through vines and branches. The farther they went, the darker it got. And the harder it became to see.

They all walked in silence. In this part of the forest, it was best not to attract attention.

Laurel had another reason for keeping quiet. She was listening for the sound of rushing water. That would tell them they were nearing the river.

All at once, Foxglove stopped in his tracks. Laurel started to ask him what was going on. But the pixie grabbed her with one hand and Primrose with the other. Roughly he dragged them into the shelter of a fallen tree.

"Shhh!" he hissed. "Someone—or something—is out there!"

CHAPTER TEN

A Familiar Footprint

ear tightened Laurel's throat until she could barely swallow. Trolls rarely roamed this side of the river. Still, she'd seen them even closer to the Dappled Woods than this.

The three waited for several minutes, listening for more sounds. Nothing. Laurel finally risked bobbing up to peer around.

A gleam in the underbrush caught her eye. As she watched, more lights flickered nearby. She could see—

"Sprites!" she hissed. "That's who's following us!"

"Great!" muttered Foxglove. "Just what we need now."

Primrose snorted. "Maybe if we ignore them, they'll go away."

It was Laurel's turn to snort. She stepped out from the bushes to face their visitors. "Peapod! Burdock!" she cried.

The two sprites stood there, grinning from ear to ear. "What are you doing here? I thought you were too frightened of trolls to come this far."

At that, the grins faded from the sprites' faces. "We are," whispered Peapod. The small sprite seemed to shrink and lose some of her shimmer.

"We came anyway," said Burdock. "Because we didn't mean to cause all this trouble."

Primrose grunted. "Of course not. It just happened to work out that way."

Burdock simply rolled his eyes. But Peapod glared at Primrose. "I still don't like you," she declared.

Laurel looked down at the little sprite. She could see the fear in Peapod's eyes. The Bogs of Bleak were the last place Laurel would have chosen to visit. But she *had* to go there. The sprites didn't. And it didn't seem in their nature to put themselves in danger. Or to think about others. Peapod and Burdock's offer was very special and very brave.

"We're glad to have your help," Laurel said softly.

"Yes," said Foxglove after a moment. "I don't know this part of the forest well."

A long silence followed as the two sprites eyed Primrose. At last the woodfairy spoke up. "I guess I'm glad to see you too."

In response, Peapod did a handstand. Burdock tickled the little sprite's feet until they both fell over.

"If you're going to help us, you have to be quiet," said Foxglove. "We're getting pretty close to the Bogs of Bleak. Can't you smell them?"

That settled the sprites down. Both slowly circled about, sniffing loudly.

"I smell something awful," said Peapod.

"Me too," admitted Burdock. "I've smelled it before. It's the trolls' bog, all right."

Foxglove nodded. "Like I said, we'll be glad to have your help. But this is dangerous. You have to do what I tell you."

Burdock nodded solemnly. Peapod's head bobbed up and down in excited agreement.

"Okay. Let's go," said Foxglove. He pushed aside a bush and headed forward. The others fell in behind him. Peapod and Laurel followed at the end of the line.

The little sprite slipped a hand into Laurel's. "I'm scared," she whispered.

"I know," responded Laurel. "I am too."

"I guess it's a good thing the dandelions grew close to the trolls' bog," added Peapod thoughtfully. "Otherwise, we'd have eaten them all up by now. Just like we ate yours." She licked her lips at the memory.

"How can you do that?" asked Laurel.

"Do what?"

"Eat all of something you find in the forest," Laurel replied.

"Why, it's easy to do. Especially when you're hungry," said Peapod. She raised an eyebrow, clearly confused by Laurel's question.

Laurel realized that Peapod didn't understand. Probably none of the sprites did. Still, she had to try to explain. "If you eat all of something, it's gone forever," she said. "You're never able to pick it again."

Peapod squinched her eyes tight, obviously trying to think. Then she smiled. "That's okay. We can always find something else to eat."

Laurel sighed. "Not forever, Peapod."

Peapod skipped along at her side for a moment in silence. "Well, Foxglove is a pixie," she said at last. "I know what pixies are like. They're scavengers. They pick up everything they find. How come you're mad at me and not at him?"

"I'm not mad at you," Laurel protested. "I'm just trying to explain something. Besides, a pixie never eats or takes everything he finds. If Foxglove discovers a tree full of acorns, he doesn't gather them all. Even though acorns are one of his favorite treats."

"What does he do then?"

"He always leaves half of what he finds. Sometimes he even buries a few."

"Why? So he can come back and eat them later?" asked Peapod.

"He doesn't ever eat those acorns," said Laurel. "He leaves them so they grow into new trees. Trees with lots more acorns on them."

She waited a moment for Peapod to think that over. Then she continued, "It's just like our dandelions. If you'd left some, they would have made seeds. Those seeds would have grown into new fairy dandelions."

Both Peapod and Laurel were quiet after that. Peapod was trying her hardest to make sense of Laurel's words. And Laurel was thinking about a world without new woodfairies.

The sound of rushing water drew Laurel from her thoughts. They were nearly there, she realized.

Gradually the dark woods opened up to sunlight—and a wide band of water.

The group stopped and looked over the scene. On this side of the river, reeds and flowers dotted the bank.

On the other side, the bank rose steep and muddy. Beyond grew a forest of short, twisted trees. There wasn't a spot of green in sight.

Laurel caught Foxglove's eye. She knew he was thinking about the last time they'd seen the Bogs of Bleak. Neither one of them wanted to cross the river again. Still, both had been preparing themselves for this.

But Primrose was another matter. Laurel saw how the other fairy stood stiffly, her arms tight against her sides.

It's even worse for Primrose than for me, thought Laurel. She's never really known much about the world beyond the peaceful Dappled Woods.

Laurel reached a decision. Primrose shouldn't have to do this. Laurel couldn't let her.

She reached out and touched Primrose's elbow. The woodfairy jumped, then shook her head as if scolding herself.

"You stay here, Primrose," suggested Laurel. "We need someone to watch this side of the river."

"I'm coming with you, Laurel," Primrose said. "I told you that before." She gave Laurel a half smile. "But thanks for trying to give me an excuse not to."

Laurel nodded, then turned to Foxglove. "How are we going to get across? You know our wings aren't strong enough to carry us that far. And even if we could fly, you and the sprites can't."

Foxglove pulled a small ax from his bag. "We're going to make a raft," he announced.

For the next hour, the group worked rapidly. Foxglove cut thick branches. Burdock dragged them to the edge of the river. Peapod searched the forest for strong vines. Laurel and Primrose used these to lash the branches together.

At last the raft was done. It was barely big enough to hold them, but it was sturdy.

Foxglove picked up several tall, thick sticks. He handed one to Burdock and another to Laurel. "You'll both need to help me pole this thing," he said. "Now let's get it in the water."

They carefully tied the raft to a tree trunk on the bank. Then, working together, they pushed it right to the water's edge.

When everyone was safely aboard, Foxglove took out his ax again.

"Hold tight!" he warned. He chopped through the vine, cutting the raft loose from the bank.

For a few moments, they bobbed there in the quiet waters. Then a push from Foxglove sent the raft out into the river.

At once the ride became rougher. The raft bobbed crazily, dipping into the water and popping back up. Primrose and Peapod clung together at the center of the raft. Laurel and Burdock followed Foxglove's shouted directions. All three poled wildly to keep the raft from going with the current straight downstream.

At last they were across. The raft thudded against the muddy shore.

"Jump!" shouted Laurel as the raft tried to skip back into the river. She led the way, leaping onto the bank with the vine rope in one hand. Quickly she tied the raft to the roots of an old tree.

The others followed, scrambling ashore. There they pulled the raft out of the water. Then they gathered moss and leaves and tossed them down onto it. By the time they finished, the little craft blended into the shoreline.

"Now if any trolls come along, they won't notice it," said Foxglove.

They headed up the steep bank. At the top, a wasteland stretched out before them. Leafless trees bent their thorny branches almost to the earth. Their dark, twisted roots made parts of the path nearly impossible to see. In addition, a gray mist rose from the ground—thick with threat. Worst of all, an overpowering smell rose from the filthy bogs all around them.

Laurel shook her head. How could anything as wonderful as the fairies' glowing dandelions grow here?

As if he'd heard her thoughts, Burdock stepped forward. "The glowing dandelions were off this way," he said, pointing to the left. "At least I think they were." He darted a glance in the opposite direction.

"Wait a minute," he said. "I guess it was this way."

"Are you sure?" asked Foxglove.

Burdock studied his surroundings once more. "Yes," he said at last. "I remember that tree. The one with that scar from a lightning bolt."

Burdock set off, with the others behind. They walked single file, alert for signs of trolls.

Before long they came upon a crude dam built across a narrow stream. Behind it was a still pool of clear blue water.

"Who built this?" Primrose asked Laurel in a whisper.

"Trolls, I suppose," Laurel answered quietly. "They don't like clean water running into their bogs. So they probably built a dam to keep this stream from flowing any farther."

They skirted the pool, heading downhill a bit. But they stopped when Foxglove held up one hand in warning. Without speaking, he pointed to a spot a few inches ahead of them. Several deep footprints could be seen in the mud.

"Claw marks," Laurel softly observed.

Foxglove nervously bit his bottom lip. "Trolls, all right. A lot of them too. In fact, I think a hunting party has been through here. I've noticed other tracks before this. And bits of rough fabric caught on thorns."

"They might head back this way then," said Laurel.

Foxglove nodded. "We'd better get out of sight."

"But we're almost to the spot where I saw the dandelions," protested Burdock. "Can't we just hurry there and get them?"

"Hurrying is a good idea," agreed Peapod. She peeked past Foxglove to eye the path ahead.

"Not if we get caught," commented Foxglove. "It's clear that this is a troll trail. So let's find some underbrush and then decide how to do our scouting."

He led the others a little farther before halting at the edge of a clearing. Pointing across the open space, he directed them to some thick bushes. "That's it," he said. "The perfect hiding place."

"It's so dark there," whispered Primrose. "Even darker than out here. Don't you think—"

"Ouch!" yelped Peapod.

Before the sprite could cry out again, Laurel locked a hand over her mouth. Peapod mumbled and tried to hop on one foot. But she could only wobble back and forth in Laurel's firm grasp.

"Shhh!" said Foxglove. "What's the matter?"

Peapod stopped hopping and pointed. There at the edge of the clearing was a dented iron pot. Its rusty surface was partly hidden in the mud and grass.

Foxglove stared open-mouthed at Peapod's find. "That does it!" he hissed. "We're not just on a troll trail! We've ended up in the middle of a campsite! It's almost sunset now. We've got to hide before they come back for the night."

No sooner had he spoken than they heard noises in the distance. Like a herd of startled deer, they all leapt into the bushes at the edge of the clearing. There they crouched, holding their breath.

The noise grew louder. The smell grew worse. Then three trolls stomped into view.

CHAPTER ELEVEN

Tricks and Trolls

he trolls were every bit as fearsome as Laurel remembered. All three had thick arms ending in clawlike fingers. Long teeth jutted from their wide mouths. And their skin was a sickly gray, all the grayer for being coated with dried mud.

Yet as Laurel took a closer look, she noticed something. These trolls weren't very big. Even the biggest of the three was smaller than most she'd seen.

Now the largest troll threw a bag down at the center of the clearing. The other two glanced sideways at him before adding their bags to the pile.

To Laurel's horror, the top bag began to wiggle madly. There was something alive in there! Most likely a small animal the trolls had trapped. She had to bite back a cry. It was so easy to recall her own terror at being trapped in a troll's net.

The two smaller trolls busied themselves building a fire. Soon thick smoke blanketed the clearing. It mixed with the odor of wet troll and rotten bog water.

With their campfire built, the trolls settled down. All three kept a stony silence at first. Then one of the smaller trolls growled at his even smaller companion.

Laurel tried to concentrate on what they were saying. Understanding them wasn't easy. But she'd done it before.

At last she began to make sense of the conversation.

"Told you so, Wart," one small troll was saying in a rough voice. "No hunting there. You should listen to me."

"Think your spot was so good, Slug?" shot back Wart.

Slug sprang to his feet, his clawed fists ready to strike. Wart crouched too, eager for a fight. The trolls began to circle one another, jabbing and poking.

With a roar, the larger troll leapt to his feet. In two steps, he'd reached the fighters. He grabbed Slug with one hand and Wart with the other. Shaking them both, he snarled, "Enough of that! Save it for tomorrow—for the hunting. *If* you want to go home, that is. Think we can go back with what we've got now? Not without a big catch to show, we can't."

He dropped them both on the ground. Slug angrily rubbed his bruised shoulder. "So you're the boss now, Gristle? Who says?"

Gristle gave Slug a dirty look. Then he stomped back to his spot, kicking the bags as he went by. One squeaked in response.

Laurel leaned close to the others. "Can you understand them, Foxglove?" she whispered.

"Most of what they say," he replied.

"How?" asked Primrose in a frightened voice. "It just sounds like grunts and snarls to me."

"It pretty much *is* grunts and snarls," said Laurel. "But the more carefully you listen, the more you understand."

"I don't want to understand," responded Primrose.

"It could be worse," Laurel told her. "These must be young trolls. Even the biggest one—Gristle—doesn't seem very old. They don't sound too sure of themselves either."

"You mean trolls get bigger than this?" asked Primrose.

"Oh yes," said Foxglove. "Much bigger. And I think Laurel's right. These three are probably out hunting on their own for the first time."

The watchers fell silent as Gristle got to his feet once more. "Time to eat!" he announced.

Slug eagerly reached for one of the bags. "Squirrel tastes good," he said. He licked his lips and started to open the bag.

Gristle swiftly cuffed the smaller troll. "Hands off!" he ordered. "We eat squirrel now and we've got nothing to show!" He pulled the drawstring shut and tossed the bag back on the ground. "It's plants tonight—and nothing else!" he declared.

Wart snatched another bag and dumped the contents onto the muddy ground. Out tumbled slimy leaves, rotted bark, and moldy mushrooms.

The trolls fell upon the plants, grabbing handfuls and stuffing them into their mouths.

At last Slug sat back and burped loudly. "Not as good as squirrel," he said sadly.

Gristle picked his teeth with a sharp twig. "Nothing like squirrel," he said.

"Wish we were home," muttered Wart. "Better eats there."

"Better eats," growled Gristle. "There'll be *no* eats if we don't go back with a good catch."

Wart plopped his hands on his hairy knees. "Maybe. Maybe not," he grumbled. Then again, "Wish we were home. Now."

Slug bit his lip. "Home," he repeated. He half-heartedly threw a stick into the fire. "Food. And good fires. And lots of other trolls. Not..."

"What!" barked Gristle, when Slug failed to finish.

"Not...scary, like this."

Gristle stared at Slug, a horrible frown wrinkling his brow. "Scary!" he snorted.

"That's right."

This time the comment came from Wart. He sneaked a glance at Gristle before lowering his head. Then both he and Slug scooted nearer the fire.

Primrose nudged Laurel. "What's happening?" she asked.

"They want to go home," Laurel reported. "They're scared."

"What?" asked Primrose in wonder. "How can something that horrible be afraid of anything?"

Laurel didn't answer. Until now, she'd never imagined it could be possible either. Still, even frightened and homesick, the trolls were dangerous.

The three trolls said little after that. Laurel and the others watched as night crept into the bogs. Though stiff and cold, they were afraid to move even in the dark. As jumpy as the trolls were, they'd likely figure out fast that they had company.

Finally three snores rose from around the campfire. Laurel sighed. At last the trolls had fallen asleep!

As Laurel quietly shifted position, her eyes caught sight of a strange glow. It wasn't the trolls' fire. This light came from beyond the clearing. And unlike the dirty, angry flames of the fire, this was soft and inviting. Just like—

Laurel gasped.

"What?" hissed Foxglove in alarm. "What's wrong?"

"Look!" whispered Laurel. She turned Foxglove's head until he was staring in the direction of the glow.

"What is that?" asked the pixie.

"I think—I hope—it's Burdock's dandelions," replied Laurel. She leaned over to tap Burdock on the shoulder.

The sprite, who'd been almost asleep, jerked upright.

"Shhh!" ordered Foxglove before Burdock could make noise.

"What's the matter?" asked Burdock sleepily.

"Look over there," said Laurel. "Past the campfire."

"Oh," said Burdock. He yawned. "That's it. Just like I told you. The dandelions."

He yawned again. "Can we go pick them? Then leave?"

"Right now?" asked Primrose fearfully. "With the trolls so close?"

"Primrose is right," sighed Laurel. "It will take a while to dig up the dandelions. The trolls could wake up before we're done. That would be—"

She broke off as a sleeping form stirred and sat up.

"Stupid light!" a rough voice snarled. It sounded like Gristle.

Against the firelight, Laurel saw the shadow of an upraised arm. Then she heard a thump.

"What?" yelped another troll as he jumped from his sleeping spot by the fire.

"Quiet, Wart!" ordered Gristle. "Only a rock. It's that light. It needs smashing."

"Stupid glow! Stupid flowers!" grumbled a third voice. "Wait until tomorrow. We'll rip 'em up. Stomp on 'em. Mash 'em into…"

The threats drifted off into a mutter, followed by a snore. In minutes, silence once again settled over the clearing.

"Did you hear that?" asked Laurel.

"What did they say?" Primrose whispered. "Is it bad?"

As Laurel explained, Primrose moaned. "It's hopeless," she said. "They'll destroy the dandelions before we can dig them up."

"Maybe they'll forget about them in the morning,"

Foxglove said hopefully.

"What if they don't?" asked Laurel. "What if—"

A sharp poke interrupted her. "Hey!" she cried softly.

"Sorry," said Burdock. "But Peapod and I have a plan."

"What kind of plan?" Foxglove asked.

"Well, you said these trolls were frightened. Right?" Burdock said.

"They seem to be," agreed Laurel.

"Then we should be able to scare them off," said Burdock. "And we know how to do it," he stated proudly.

"How?" asked Laurel, Foxglove, and Primrose in one voice.

"We'll play tricks on them!" said Peapod happily. "We'll get them all mixed up!"

"I don't know," said Laurel slowly. "They could figure out what's going on. Then they'd come after us."

"You might just make them mad," added Primrose.

Burdock puffed out his chest. "These trolls aren't smart enough to figure anything out."

They all eyed the sleeping trolls, as if the trio would answer for themselves. Finally Foxglove spoke up. "You know, it could work. They're pretty nervous already. I don't think it would take too much to chase them off. Then we can dig up the dandelions and get out of here."

Laurel added her vote. "Okay. Let's try it." She studied Primrose, who slowly nodded her agreement.

Peapod grinned in delight. "Yes!" she giggled. "And since it was my idea, I get to say what we do first."

Laurel gently laid her hand on Peapod's arm. "I have an idea too, Peapod." Before the little sprite could protest, Laurel continued. "Please, it's important. Before we do anything else, we have to free the animals they've caught."

"Oh," said Peapod. "I didn't think of that. Okay. It's not much of a trick, though. So you do it. Burdock and I'll get ready for a really good mischief."

The two sprites slipped away, hardly making a sound.

"I'll help you, Laurel," said Foxglove. "Primrose, you can keep watch for us."

As softly as possible, Laurel and Foxglove pushed past the bushes into the clearing. They tiptoed around the sleeping trolls and over to the hunting bags.

Laurel leaned close. "Don't make a sound," she whispered to the trapped animals. "We're friends. Here to free you."

She reached out and picked up the top bag. She quickly untied it while Foxglove did the same with another bag.

A squirrel jumped out of the bag Laurel held. It whispered a quick thank-you, and ran for the forest. In short order, they'd freed all the animals.

Laurel and Foxglove went back across the clearing. Again they were careful not to make a sound. But as they passed Gristle, he suddenly began thrashing.

Laurel and Foxglove froze—which ended up being the wrong thing to do. Gristle rolled over, pinning Foxglove's foot to the ground. The pixie gasped in fear and turned a white face to his friend.

Laurel looked around anxiously. Her eyes lit on a stick, and she snatched it up. Then she lightly ran it along the troll's thick arm.

Still asleep, Gristle swatted at the stick as if it were a pesky insect. At last he rolled away from Foxglove.

The pixie took off for the underbrush with Laurel right on his heels.

They found the sprites and Primrose waiting for them. "That was close!" Burdock observed.

"Too close!" replied Foxglove.

"Well, we know how to get back at them," Peapod said. She dipped a hand into her pocket and pulled out a fistful of acorns. "We found these where a squirrel buried them. Now we'll drop them on the trolls' heads!" She laughed merrily.

"Shhh!" ordered Burdock. "Be quiet or they'll be dropping *us* on our heads!"

Peapod settled down. With a nod, Burdock led her out into the clearing. The others remained in the bushes, straining to hear.

There was a squishy sound—a foot sinking into mud. A soft giggle, quickly silenced, followed. Next a series of plopping sounds. Then—

"Ouch! Stop that!"

"Wasn't me, Slug! Let go!"

"Hit me, will you?"

"Ow! My nose!"

Woodfairies and pixie crept closer. In the faint firelight, they saw the trolls rolling around on the ground. Wild blows and handfuls of mud flew back and forth. It was lucky the three were busy shouting at one another. Otherwise, they might have heard Peapod's laughter.

Finally the trolls broke off the fight. Complaining and blaming one another, they went back to their sleeping spots.

However, the sprites weren't finished. The campfire went out, mysteriously buried by dirt. Wart whimpered in the darkness until Gristle bellowed at him.

When the three seemed ready to doze off again, the sprites attacked once more. Laurel watched in alarm as

Peapod and Burdock crept forward and tickled the trolls' feet. But before they could be seen, the two sprites darted away. Another round of blows and insults followed.

So it went for the rest of the night. No one—troll, fairy, pixie, or sprite—got much sleep.

As the sky began to lighten, the red-eyed trolls stumbled to their feet. It didn't take long for them to discover the rest of the sprites' tricks.

Slug reached for a jug and wearily took a drink. At once his eyes bugged out in horror. "Fah!" he shouted, spitting out the mouthful he'd taken. "What's this slop? *Fresh* water? Where's my swamp water?"

"Hey!" yelled Gristle at the same moment. "Our catch is gone!"

Slug dropped his water jug. He and Wart ran toward Gristle and the pile of hunting bags.

Charges of not tying the bags shut were followed by punches and curses. Then all three started kicking the bags across the clearing.

"I think we've done it," whispered Laurel. "They're sure to take off for home now."

The trolls continued to quarrel. But they showed no sign of packing up and moving out.

At last the three trolls settled into a heap, breathing heavily. "Can't ever go home now," moaned Slug.

"Never," echoed Wart. "Not with no catch to show."

Gristle smacked Wart before adding his own grumble. "Great hunters. Not a chance we'll be called that now. Not us. Can't make a fire burn all night. Can't keep our catches. Can't even keep our water nice and dirty."

Wart and Slug tipped back their heads and howled.

Gristle gazed around the clearing. "Better get used to this, I guess. Have to stay here. Start a new village. From now on, this is home."

At that, Gristle broke down too and howled as loudly as the other trolls.

Laurel wanted to add her own wails to the terrible noise. How would they ever get the dandelions if the trolls didn't leave?

Peapod crept to her side. "They'd might not notice us if we ran past them now. We could grab the dandelions."

Laurel shook her head. "We can't just pull the plants up. We have to get them roots and all. Otherwise, they'll just die. Even if we carry them back to the Dappled Woods safely."

"Oh," said Peapod. "I didn't think of that."

At this point, a fresh fight broke out among the trolls. This one made all the quarrels before seem like play. For over an hour, the three fought, screamed, and snarled at one another. Once Gristle and Slug almost tumbled into the bushes where Laurel and the others hid. Fortunately the trolls rolled back out again just as quickly.

Finally the fighters wore themselves out. They crawled back to the dead fire and glared at each other.

"I don't want to live here," sniffed Wart. He wiped his dirty face with his even dirtier hand. "Too close to the river. The smell of fresh water makes me sick."

"You'll be guzzling it for breakfast every day if you don't quiet down!" grunted Gristle.

Laurel sat back as an idea suddenly struck her. "That's it!" she whispered. "I know how we can get the trolls out of here!"

CHAPTER TWELVE

A Fresh Idea

aurel motioned to the others. "Come on," she said. "Back the way we came."

"We're leaving?" asked Peapod hopefully.

"Just to make plans," Laurel told her.

Silently they retraced their steps. Halfway to the river, Foxglove stopped. "Okay, Laurel," he said. "What's your idea?"

In reply, Laurel asked a question. "What do trolls fear more than anything?"

It was Primrose who answered. "Rushing water," she said, sounding confused. She remembered Laurel's story of her earlier escape from the bogs. How she'd been safe once she was on the other side of the river.

"I don't see how knowing that helps us," Primrose added. "The trolls aren't camped that close to the river. And that's the only rushing water around here."

"I thought we might make some for them," said Laurel.

"I get it," said Foxglove. He grinned at Peapod and Burdock. "You two will like this. It's mischief time."

"Well, I don't get it, Laurel," said Primrose. "So tell me."

"Remember the dammed-up stream we passed?"

"Yes. So—" Understanding flooded Primrose's face. "Oh!" she gasped.

Peapod began to jump excitedly. "We'll bust their dam," she caroled. "We'll break it open!"

"And since the trolls' campsite is lower than the dam and pond—" said Laurel.

Foxglove finished for her. "Once the dam goes, the water will shoot right into their camp! It's fresh water too. They'll hate it!"

Peapod did a back flip and knocked Burdock off his feet.

By the time the two sprites had picked themselves up, the other three were huddled together. Before long their plans were made.

The friends decided to try their idea at once. It was light enough to see what they were doing. The dam was also far enough from the campsite that the trolls wouldn't spot them.

Back at the dam, they quickly began moving rocks and branches. The structure was roughly built, so it wasn't hard to take apart. However, the rocks and branches were large—and heavy. It took all five of them to lift some.

As they worked, water began to trickle down the face of the dam. It formed little streams, all seeking lower ground.

Yet it was merely trickles of water. Hardly enough to scare the young trolls away.

Foxglove straightened up and wiped his brow. "This isn't going to do it," he sighed. "There's no way we can lift the really big stuff at the bottom of the dam. Unless we do that, most of the water will stay right here."

"I could jump on the branches," suggested Peapod.

"That won't help," said Laurel with a shake of her head. "You don't weigh very much, Peapod."

"It would be fun," sighed the sprite. "More fun than lifting things."

Silence greeted Peapod's complaint. The others sat down to rest while they studied the situation.

A sudden thought brought Laurel back to her feet. "Primrose!" she exclaimed. "Do you remember the story the Eldest read from the Chronicles last year? About the time the huge rock fell?"

Primrose's eyes lit up. "I'd forgotten about that! You're right, Laurel!"

In an instant, Primrose was on her feet too. The wood-fairies began searching the area.

"It has to be fairly long," Primrose said.

"And thick," added Laurel. "So it won't break."

"What are you two talking about?" asked Foxglove. "What did it say in the Chronicles?"

Laurel paused. "A long time ago, a huge rock fell from the top of a cliff. It landed in the middle of a stream that runs through the Dappled Woods. The stream was blocked and the water backed up. That flooded everything nearby."

Primrose took up the story. "The fairies couldn't move the rock. Not until someone came up with a good idea. They stuck one end of a big log under the rock. Then everyone pushed down on the other end."

"Of course!" Foxglove cried. "A lever! Why didn't I think of that?"

The pixie joined the search. Soon they found what they needed: the trunk of a fallen pine. Long and straight, it was the perfect lever.

"Come on," ordered Laurel. "It's going to take all five of us."

By rolling and pushing, they got the log into position. One end went under the branches and rocks at the bottom of the dam. The other stuck up at an angle.

"Okay," said Foxglove. "We'll all have to put our weight on the high end."

"Just be ready to jump out of the way when the dam breaks," Laurel reminded them.

There were nods of understanding. They all leaned on the angled end, pressing down carefully and steadily.

At first nothing happened. Then, ever so slowly, the free end of the log began to move downward.

Even more slowly, the other end began to rise. Along with it came the huge branches that formed the bottom of the dam. Rocks tumbled aside as the branches lifted.

The trickle became a stream. Then the pile of branches gave a final shudder. With a whoosh of water, the dam broke apart.

At once the log began to fall from under them. "Jump!" shouted Laurel.

Foxglove pushed Burdock and Peapod toward safety as he leapt clear. At the same time, the two woodfairies fluttered into the air.

In seconds, all five were safely out of reach of the gushing water. Gasping for breath, they watched as the pond quickly emptied.

For a moment, they rested. But then they heard the sound of shouts and curses from the clearing.

"I think it worked!" hissed Foxglove. "Let's go and check!"

They didn't slow until they'd almost reached the trolls' camp. Foxglove led the way to their old hiding spot at the edge of the clearing. There they lay on their stomachs and took in the scene before them.

The clearing had become a shining lake. A large rock formed an island in the lake's center. And that's where the three trolls had taken shelter.

In the face of this new disaster, Wart broke down. He forgot about being a tough hunter and melted into a little troll. Tipping back his head, he wailed, "Home! I want to go home!"

Gristle smacked the smaller troll, almost knocking him into the water. Wart settled into a crouch, sniffing loudly.

Slug seemed about to add his own sad cry. But after casting nervous glances from Gristle to the pond, he kept his mouth shut.

"Fah! What a stink!" muttered Gristle.

Laurel fought back a laugh. "The stream washed away the swamp water," she whispered.

"It smells better to me," commented Primrose.

"But not to the trolls," said Laurel.

Now they played a waiting game. The friends watched the trolls, who watched the water. From time to time, the trolls burst into snarls and sobs. However, there was little they could do to rescue themselves.

In the end, it was nature that decided things. As the water spread out, the level of the lake slowly dropped. Before long there was only a knee-deep pool left in the clearing. But it was clear that the water was there to stay.

"What do we do now?" whined Wart.

"Have to go in there," said Slug. He observed the shiny water uneasily. "If we want to get out of here."

"Can't do that! It's...it's clean!" howled Wart.

"Right!" Gristle shouted. "I've had my fill of you!"

He gave a fierce shove, sending Wart tumbling into the water. Then Gristle stepped off the rock and onto Wart.

"Hey!" shouted the smaller troll, grabbing for an ankle. Gristle just pushed him aside. He waded through the water, looking disgusted.

At the far side of the clearing, where it was drier, Gristle turned back. "Come on," he snarled to Wart and Slug. "Time to go home."

Wart lifted his dripping head hopefully. "Home?"

Gristle shrugged. "Catch or no catch, we can't stay here."

That was enough for Slug. Holding his nose, he jumped into the water and waded over to Gristle. "What about the dam?" he asked. "Should we tell 'em it broke?"

"That's a good one!" snarled Gristle. "We say it broke, they'll be wanting us to fix it. Want to work here, do you? Smell this all day?" He waved his hand at the shining pool.

Slug wrinkled his nose. "Dam's just fine. Nothing's broke," he replied.

He and Gristle gathered up their bags and stomped into the forest.

Wart stared after them, still trying to understand what was going on. Suddenly he jumped to his feet. "Wait for me!" he shouted. Snatching his bag, he splashed through the water. In moments, not a troll could be seen.

Laurel and the others waited a minute to be sure the trolls were gone. Then Laurel motioned to the others. "Come on! Let's get the dandelions!"

They raced out from the underbrush and waded across the clearing. Once they reached the other side, the dandelions were easy to spot. Like the ones in Moonlight Meadow, these flowers were larger than normal. And even in the daylight, a soft glow surrounded each flower head.

"Be careful," Laurel instructed. "We have to dig around the roots. Then lift them out."

Following Laurel's example, the others grabbed flat rocks and began to dig. Soon a dozen great flowers lay on the grass.

"That's enough," Laurel decided.

"But there are still more dandelions!" protested Peapod.

"No," said Laurel firmly. "We have to leave some to make seeds. Remember?"

Peapod put a hand to her mouth. "Oh. So new dandelions can grow, right?" she said. Laurel nodded and Peapod grinned.

Foxglove took off his cloak and laid it on the ground. "Pile the dandelions on here," he said. "My scavenging bag isn't big enough for all of these."

The dandelions were soon safely packed away. Foxglove tied a rope around the top of the cloak and stepped back.

"Home?" he asked Laurel.

She nodded and smiled a tired smile. "Home," she repeated.

They took turns carrying the dandelion-filled cloak. It was hard going in parts of the muddy bog. But they finally reached the river. They were relieved to find their raft still there, safely hidden.

Laurel didn't breathe easily until the dandelions were on board and the raft was in the river. I hope I never see the Bogs of Bleak again, she thought.

The current snatched them away. Once more they battled its pull. Once more they made it to the other side.

After the dandelions were unloaded, the two sprites said their farewells. "We're glad you found more dandelions," said

Burdock. "Now it's time we were going." He grinned at Peapod. "We have quite a tale to tell the others."

"I'll miss you, Laurel," added Peapod. "You saved my life." Then she studied Primrose. "So did you. I think you must like me."

For a moment, Primrose just stared at the sprite. Finally she smiled. "A little," she said.

"Then I like you a little too." Peapod giggled and set off down the trail.

With a wave, Burdock fell in step beside her. Laurel and her friends watched as the sprites headed down the path. Beside a bare spot in the woods, Peapod suddenly stopped. She felt in her pocket, pulled something out, and bent over. After scraping a hole in the dirt, she planted her treasure.

Straightening up, she shouted, "Laurel! That was one of my leftover acorns. Now it will be a tree!"

With that, the sprite skipped several steps and darted into the bushes. Burdock followed. There was a shimmer of light. Then that too disappeared.

Foxglove grinned. "I guess Peapod did listen to you."

"She'll forget soon enough," remarked Primrose.

"Maybe," Laurel said. "Maybe not. The sprites are full of surprises."

The trio headed homeward. Tired as they were, they stopped only to water the wilting plants. By early evening, they neared the Dappled Woods.

As they got closer, Laurel grew more nervous. "What if this doesn't work?" she worried aloud. "What if the dandelions don't live? Or if they do, but no fairies appear?"

"Oh, stop it, Laurel," said Primrose. Then she gently touched Laurel's arm. "No matter what, you tried to fix things.

You have to remember that."

Startled by the other fairy's words, Laurel merely nodded.

At last they reached the edge of the Dappled Woods. To their surprise, most of the woodfairies were waiting there for them. Chitters and Mistletoe sat nearby.

"Laurel?" the Eldest asked, looking hopefully at the heavy cloak.

"These aren't the dandelions from our meadow, Eldest. But they glow just like ours. Maybe they'll work."

"We'll have to hope so," said the Eldest softly. "Well done, all of you. Now let's get them to the meadow."

In silence the pixie and all the woodfairies hurried to the meadow. There Laurel saw that the other fairies had readied things. The soil had been raked smooth. Deep holes had been dug for the new dandelions. Full watering cans stood ready.

Soon all twelve dandelions were planted and watered. Foxglove and the fairies stood back and studied the results of their work. It wasn't a hopeful picture. The dandelions drooped sadly, their heads almost touching the soil.

"I don't know," murmured Laurel.

"No, you don't," agreed the Eldest. "None of us knows if this will work. But at least now we have hope. We'll just have to wait and see what happens."

Sighing, the old fairy headed back toward the Ancient Clearing. The others followed her—all but two who remained behind to guard the meadow.

Laurel took one last look at the dandelions. "Grow strong," she whispered.

CHAPTER THIRTEEN

Dandelions by Moonlight

**M**oonlight slanted through the trees, lighting the fairy meadow. A soft wind had begun to blow. It stirred the long grass and violets—and the twelve dandelions at the center of the meadow. Their glowing heads danced, creating a circle of bobbing, golden lights.

Now a line of woodfairies approached. Each carried a small candlelit lantern, adding more tiny sparks of light.

Laurel shivered in nervous excitement. This night would determine the future of the woodfairies. Would the dandelions bring forth another group of newborns?

Laurel thought about the past week. She'd been so relieved when the dandelions began to recover from their uprooting. She and the other young fairies had made many trips to the meadow to water the flowers. Each day the dandelions had stood a little taller and become a little more firmly rooted.

At last the Eldest announced that they'd go ahead with plans for the Welcoming Ceremony. So, as they'd always done, each young fairy made a headwreath and garland for a newcomer.

Tonight Laurel and Primrose stood next to the poles bearing the wreaths and garlands. It was to be their duty—and honor—to hand these to the newborns.

As always, Primrose looked perfect. Yet somehow that didn't bother Laurel tonight. She smiled, thinking of what Ivy had said just this morning.

"So is Primrose your new best friend?" Ivy had asked with a grin.

Laurel had laughed. "*You're* my best friend," she'd replied. "You always will be. I'm still not quite perfect enough for Primrose. But at least we get along now. Most of the time."

And they did. Primrose had even helped Laurel finish her dress for the ceremony. Of course, she'd mentioned something about Laurel's messy sewing basket. However, she'd smiled as she'd said it. Then Primrose had carefully attached the soft petals of fabric that made up Laurel's skirt. She'd even complimented Laurel on the design of the dress.

Laurel's thoughts returned to the present as the other fairies entered the meadow. Quietly they filed in, forming a great circle around the dandelions.

Each fairy lowered her lantern, placing it in front of her. Then they all joined hands and waited.

The moon climbed steadily in the night sky. As it moved, the angle of its rays changed. Bit by bit, a pool of light swept across the meadow toward the dandelions.

All at once, the breeze dropped and a hushed silence fell. The moonlight washed over one of the dandelions. Then another and another.

The waiting fairies began to sing. Their song was one that hadn't been heard since the year of Laurel's birth.

As music and moonlight mingled, the dandelions began to stir. The glowing light surrounding each flower expanded. At last one of the great flower heads began to open.

Slowly the long golden petals uncurled. And as a finger of moonlight touched the flower's golden center, a diamond of light sparkled. For a moment, it burned brightly. Then it vanished. And in its place could be seen a tiny fairy.

The little creature stretched out wings as clear as glass. Once, twice she fluttered them before finally taking to the air.

Now all around the meadow, dandelions were opening. As moonlight touched each flower, other sparks of light appeared. And other tiny, perfectly formed woodfairies took flight.

Soon a dozen new fairies were in the air. As they flew, their wings became more solid and their bodies grew. In a matter of seconds, each was almost Laurel's size.

In an age-old tradition, the fairies flew straight for the flowered poles. As she watched them approach, Laurel whispered to Primrose. "They're so graceful! Do you think we were too?"

"Yes," said Primrose. Then she smiled. "Even you."

One by one, the new fairies alighted in front of Laurel and Primrose. Each received her headwreath and garland.

One by one, they moved on to be greeted by the Eldest. To each new fairy, the Eldest repeated the familiar words: "With all our hearts, we welcome you. You are one of us. Live here in peace and beauty."

After that the Eldest gave each a name: Lilac, Larkspur, Holly, Rose…

Then the newborns joined the circle. Each took a place next to a fairy who had been born the last time this mystery occurred.

Finally the last fairy stepped before Laurel. As Laurel placed a wreath on the curly head, the youngster gazed at her with bright, dancing eyes.

The Eldest gave this last newborn her name: Lily. The new

fairy took her place in the circle—next to Laurel. But Lily's curiosity was clearly too great even for this solemn moment. She twisted about to study the meadow—and knocked her headwreath to one side.

Laurel smiled to herself. I wonder if Lily's going to be at all like me, she thought. I wonder if she's a little different too. If so, maybe I can help her.

Once again the fairies began to sing. Now twelve fresh voices joined the chorus. Laurel wasn't sure, but she thought Lily's might be a tiny bit out of tune.

As their song rose over the meadow, Laurel's eyes settled on the glowing dandelions. She knew that in a few days, these petals would fall off. The dandelions would become fluffy white clouds of seeds. When the winds came, the seeds would float away. Each one would find a spot to root in the shelter of Moonlight Meadow.

Then, years from now, new fairy dandelions would bloom. The fairies would stand in this meadow again. Together, they would greet yet another generation of woodfairies.

And Laurel would be there.

More to Explore

For the Welcoming Ceremony, Laurel and the other wood-fairies made many special gifts. Have fun trying your own woodland projects to keep or give as gifts.

Woodland Welcome Candles

The fairies made candles for the lanterns used to welcome the newborns. You can create lovely woodland lights too by decorating everyday candles.

To make the candles described below, you *must* have an adult partner. If you choose to work alone, see the alternate directions that begin on page 103.

What you need

- Clean, empty coffee can
- 3-quart saucepan
- Water
- Paraffin (sold with canning supplies)
- Old newspapers
- Clean, empty tuna fish can
- Small flowers and leaves, pressed and dried (See note at the right.)
- Assorted solid color candles
- Small paintbrush

Pressed Flowers

If you don't already have pressed and dried flowers and leaves, you can make some in advance. You will need two pieces of thick cardboard, paper towels, and a pile of books. Place one piece of cardboard on a flat surface. Put two or three layers of paper toweling on top of the cardboard. Place small leaves and flowers on top of the paper towels. (Leave room between them.) Cover with two or three more paper towels, then with the second piece of cardboard. Stack the pile of books on top, and leave for about a week.

What you do

1. Put the coffee can inside the saucepan. Then fill the pan about half full of water. Add a block of paraffin to the coffee can. Ask your adult partner to melt the paraffin on the stove. It has to be watched carefully because it can burn. And never melt paraffin directly— it must be in a can with water around it.

2. Spread several layers of newspaper over your work area. Put the tuna fish can on the paper.

3. Have your adult partner pour some of the paraffin into the tuna fish can. Then turn off the stove. The hot water in the saucepan will keep the remaining paraffin melted.

4. Select a candle to decorate. Hold it steady with one hand. With the other hand, place a leaf or flower where you want on the side of the candle. (Most candles are waxy enough that your decoration should stick to the surface for a few moments.)

5. Continue to hold the candle steady with one hand. With the other, dip a paintbrush in the melted paraffin. Quickly dab a little paraffin on the edges of the flower or leaf to hold it in place.

6. Brush a thin layer of paraffin all over the flower or leaf. Allow it to dry before adding other flowers or leaves. (If the paraffin on the paintbrush dries, just dip the brush in the melted paraffin for a moment or two.)

7. Set the candle aside to dry completely while you help your partner clean up. The paintbrush will need to be thrown away or saved for making candles in the future. (The paraffin won't wash out.) Let any leftover paraffin harden in the can. Then throw the can away or save it to melt and use the paraffin again.

8. Use or display your candles. If you decide to burn them, be sure an adult is present. And put them on a saucer that will catch the melting wax. You don't need to worry about the decorative leaves and flowers. They'll just shrivel up as the candle burns.

Alternate directions: Cut-paper decorations

If you choose to work alone, decorate plain candles with flowers and leaves cut from paper. Just follow the directions below.

1. Cut out a variety of small pictures of flowers and leaves from old magazines, stationery, or wrapping paper.

2. Spread newspaper over your work area.

3. Pour some clear-drying craft glue into a saucer or bowl. Add a little water so the glue is the thickness of paint.

4. Select a candle and several cut-out decorations. Hold the candle steady with one hand. With the other hand, "paint" a layer of glue over the area to be decorated.

5. Position the cut-outs where you want them. Overlap two pieces if you choose to.

6. Wait about one minute. Then use a damp sponge to carefully dab the extra glue off the candle and the paper cut-out. (Don't worry if you can't get it all; it will dry clear.)

7. Set the candle aside to dry. When one section of a candle is completely dry, you can decorate another part.

8. Display your finished candles. However, these candles are for decoration only. Do NOT burn them.

Fairy Garland

Create a beautiful fairy garland of your own—out of crepe paper! You can choose the colors and petal shapes you want. Best of all, your flowers will never wilt or die.

What you need

- 1 yard green grosgrain ribbon (1 to 1½" wide)

- Scissors

- Crepe paper streamers in your choice of colors

- Ruler

- Floral wire (fabric-covered is best)

- Tape or marker

What you do

1. Cut a notch at each end of the ribbon as shown below. Set the ribbon aside while you make your flowers.

2. Make flowers one at a time. For each blossom, cut ten to twelve 5" strips of crepe paper.

3. Stack several strips on top of each other. Then cut triangular sections out of the middle, as shown. Continue until all strips have been cut.

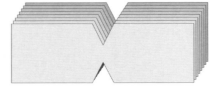

105

4. Shape the petals by trimming the strips of crepe paper in one of the ways shown below. You can stack and cut three or four strips at a time if you want.

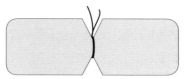

Style 1   Style 2   Style 3

5. Cut an 8" length of floral wire. Stack 10 to 12 trimmed strips and twist the wire tightly around the center, as shown.

6. Spread the petals apart to create a flower. For a special touch, roll individual petals around a pencil to curl them. You can also stretch the crepe paper slightly to round the petals. (Don't stretch the Style 3 petals; they're too thin.)

7. Lay out the ribbon on a flat surface. Place the flowers along the edge of the ribbon. Once you've decided where you want each flower, mark its spot on the ribbon with a piece of tape or a marker.

8. Attach the flowers by twisting the loose wire ends around the ribbon. Trim the ends of the wire to about ¾". Twist the ends together and tuck them under the flower.

9. Use your garland to decorate your room. Drape it on the corner of a mirror or door, the top of your computer, or around a doorknob.

Just for fun

Make a fairy garland for a favorite doll. Use a 10" length of ½"-wide ribbon as the base. Cut six to eight 3" strips of crepe paper for each flower. Follow the steps above to make miniature flowers. Then attach them to the ribbon and drape it around your doll's neck.

Dappled Woods Terrarium

What better gift to give a nature-lover than a real "wood-land" in miniature? Make a bottle garden, or terrarium, as a gift for a friend or relative. Then make one for yourself too.

What you need

- Clean, empty glass jar with a screw-on lid (a mayonnaise jar works well)
- Small pebbles or gravel
- Ruler
- Potting soil
- Long-handled wooden spoon
- Small plants (Use purchased houseplants or plants dug up from the yard. Even weeds look great in a terrarium!)
- Water

What you do

1. Put a layer of pebbles or gravel in the bottom of the jar. This layer should be at least 1" deep. The bigger the jar, the deeper the layer should be.

2. Add a layer of potting soil. The soil should be deeper than the pebbles or gravel.

3. Plan your garden. Think about how you want the plants arranged. For example, the tallest plants should go in the middle so they don't hide smaller ones.

108

4. Use a wooden spoon to make a hole for the first plant. Be sure the hole is large enough so the plant's roots fit. Place the plant into the hole and cover the roots completely.

5. Continue planting until your garden is done. Plants can be fairly close together, but leave some room for growth.

6. Sprinkle about ¼ cup water over your garden. Then screw the lid on the jar.

7. If you're giving your terrarium as a gift, make a note card with care instructions. Terrariums are great for busy people because they basically look after themselves. The plants pull water from the soil through their roots and give off water through their leaves. You don't need to do anything—unless you notice a problem.

General care hints

- If a lot of water collects on the surface of the jar, it's too wet inside. Just take the lid off for about an hour.

- If the plants inside start to wilt, it's too dry. Remove the lid, add a little water, and replace the lid.

- Don't put the terrarium in direct sunlight or the plants will "cook."

Stardust Story Sampler

Stardust Classics books feature other heroines to believe in. Come explore with Kat the Time Explorer and Alissa, Princess of Arcadia. Here are short selections from their books.

Selection from

KAT AND THE MISSING NOTEBOOKS

"Watch out, Jessie!" cried Kat. She grabbed her aunt's arm and dragged her to safety.

"Thanks," said Jessie, her face pale. "That was way too close!" She stared at the horse that had almost trampled her. Then she turned with Kat to study their surroundings.

They were in a large city, that much was clear. Huge stone buildings enclosed a paved central square. A tall tower seemed to sprout from the top of one building. Across from it, a second tower stood guard. An enormous dome filled the skyline, the building beneath it hidden by others.

The man who'd almost run over Jessie was part of a long, winding parade. Like a huge corkscrew, it curled its way into the center of the square.

Kat noted the rich clothing the onlookers wore. Her eyes went from their finery to her own. In her long, flowing dress, Kat looked like the other girls in the crowd.

"Wherever we are, it's a time before jeans were popular," noted Kat.

"Long before," agreed Jessie. "I'd say we've gone back several centuries. And I think we're in Italy. The language we're hearing—and speaking ourselves—sounds like Italian to me."

Kat turned her attention back to the square. "So you think we're in Italy hundreds of years ago?" she asked.

Jessie nodded. "The fifteenth or sixteenth century, I'd guess. A pretty exciting time—during the Renaissance."

"The Renaissance," repeated Kat. Words and images from her history classes flashed through her mind. Galileo may be alive, she thought. Or Michelangelo. Or Leonardo da Vinci.

Before long the tail end of the procession had passed by. "Thank goodness," said Kat, stepping away from the wall. "Now we can move around a bit."

They began to stroll along the edge of the square. Though the parade had broken up, there was still a bustle of activity. Peddlers pushed wheeled carts filled with fresh vegetables. Merchants sold cloth, pottery, and glassware from tables set outside the arched doorways of their shops.

Suddenly a group of young men burst from a building. Kat and Jessie stopped to watch as two of them paired off. Each youth stood on one of his partner's feet. Then they began to strike out at one another. However, they could only move a short distance with one foot pinned.

Three other strollers stopped to watch as well. "A boxing match!" a curly-haired boy announced. His voice danced with excitement. "Who do you think will win, Papa?"

The bearded man with him just shrugged. "I have no idea, Pietro. These young fools are wasting their energy. They could be better occupied." As he spoke, he tucked the leather case he was carrying under one arm.

Then out of the corner of one eye, Kat noticed another person draw closer. The tall, thin figure wore a sweeping cloak. A hat hid the upper part of his face.

The newcomer drifted closer to the man and boy. Without

warning, a hand snaked out and snatched the man's leather case. Then the dark figure dashed past Kat and Jessie, heading across the square.

"Thief!" cried the man. "Stop him! Someone stop him!"

Without thinking, Kat set off to do just that.

Selection from

ALISSA'S TOURNAMENT TROUBLES

"Why do we have to stay in my room?" complained Alissa. "I'd much rather be outside, where all the excitement is."

From her window she could see the bright banners and tents of the tournament. Visitors had come from near and far. Most of them were now living in tents just outside the castle.

That's where Alissa wanted to be too. However, the choice wasn't hers. As a princess, she had responsibilities. Her father was busy meeting with other rulers. So Alissa would greet today's guests—Lady Rosalind and her father, Baron Hubert.

"I wish they'd get here. Then we could go outside. I'm too excited about the tournament to sit around like a proper lady."

"I'm excited too," Lia admitted. "Especially after meeting all the knights. I think Sir Nicholas is the handsomest of all."

"Who cares about that, Lia?" asked Alissa. "What matters is that he's strong and brave. I'm sure he'll win the joust."

"I hope so," said Lia. "And then, after the tournament, we'll celebrate his marriage to Rosalind."

That set Alissa off. "Snake's slippers! I'm tired of hearing about this wedding. Why do they have to get married here?"

"Really, Alissa," said a stern voice.

Alissa turned to see Great-aunt Matilda at the door. As usual, her her thin lips were pinched in disapproval. Great-aunt Maude trailed along behind her.

"You know perfectly well why the wedding is taking place here," Matilda continued. "The boy's father was one of Arcadia's most loyal knights. When he lay dying, he begged your father to watch over his son. Edmund has certainly done so. He arranged for Nicholas to serve as a squire to Baron Hubert. Now Nicholas has become a knight."

"And he fell in love with Rosalind, the baron's daughter," said Lia. "It's so romantic. It will be a beautiful wedding."

"For some people," muttered Alissa.

"That's quite enough, Alissa," said her great-aunt firmly.

Then trumpets sounded from the courtyard below. "The baron's party is here," Matilda announced. "We must go."

The two girls followed the great-aunts downstairs to the castle courtyard. They'd barely stepped into place when the visitors rode up. Standard bearers led the way. Then came several well-dressed ladies. Behind them rode Baron Hubert, his bald head gleaming in the sunshine. At his side was a lovely young woman. She has to be Rosalind, thought Alissa.

Suddenly Maude said, "There's Osbert, Matilda.

Lia whispered to Alissa. "Who's Osbert?"

"Oh, just one of Baron Hubert's knights," said Alissa.

"Will we see him joust?" asked Lia.

"Osbert?" repeated Alissa. "I don't think so. He's ancient."

She pointed to a figure with wispy gray hair and a drooping mustache. His thin shoulders slumped, and he had a hint of a pot belly. Osbert was hardly the picture of a brave knight.

Matilda drew Alissa's mind back to business. "It's time we welcomed our guests," she said.

So, trying to remember what she'd been taught, Alissa greeted the visitors in her father's name.

"Now, I'm sure you all want to rest," Matilda announced. "I'll have someone show you to your chambers."

Soon only Osbert remained. He approached slowly. A blush started at his bony neck and slowly worked its way up.

"Er-er-er, greetings, Lady Matilda," he said. "You are as lovely...Er, I mean, you are the picture of...That is—"

Matilda broke in. "It is good to see you, Osbert. I'll have one of the pages show you where to set up your tent."

With a nod, she swept off. Maude trailed after her.

"How sweet," murmured Lia.

Alissa stared blankly at her friend. "Sweet?" she repeated.

"Yes," said Lia. "I mean Osbert being in love with your great-aunt Matilda."

"Osbert? In love?" sputtered Alissa. "With Matilda? Lia, don't be ridiculous!"

"Didn't you listen to him?" said Lia. "Or watch him?"

Alissa recalled Osbert's greeting to Matilda. Impossible as it seemed, the clues were all there.

Suddenly her brain began to work overtime. She was no longer thinking of the upcoming tournament. She was thinking about what it might mean if Matilda knew of Osbert's love.

Surely there was a way to help things along...

STARDUST CLASSICS titles are written under pseudonyms. Authors work closely with Margaret Hall, executive editor of Kid Galaxy, Inc.

Ms. Hall has devoted her professional career to working with and for children. She has a B.S. and an M.S. in education from the State University of New York at Geneseo. For many years, she taught as a classroom and remedial reading teacher for students from preschool through upper elementary. Ms. Hall has also served as an editor with an educational publisher and as a consultant for the Iowa State Department of Education. She has a long history as a freelance writer for the school market, authoring several children's books as well as numerous teacher resources.

Robert Rodriguez, illustrator of *Laurel and the Sprites' Mischief,* is a native of New Orleans, Louisiana. Since graduating from Choinard Art Institute, Mr. Rodriguez has won numerous awards for his work. His art has been featured on movie posters for *The Jewel of the Nile* and *City Slickers II* as well as on the covers of books, magazines, videos, and record albums. He has also created paintings for Ringling Brothers Circus, Superbowl XXVI, and other clients.

Mr. Rodriguez's canvases have even included entire buildings! He was commissioned to paint a giant wall mural on the side of a building in downtown Los Angeles. The mural celebrated soccer, Latinos, and the 1998 World Cup. It was on display from April through August of 1998.

Recently Mr. Rodriguez received international praise as the painter of the Cinco de Mayo postage stamp. This stamp was released simultaneously by the United States and Mexican Postal Services. It is part of the U.S. Postal Service's Holiday Celebration stamp series. He is currently working on a group of paintings for stamps in the Celebrate the Century Series.

This Book Is Just the Beginning…

Order the new iDolls catalog to discover an entire fantasy world beyond the Stardust Classic stories. The Stardust collection includes beautiful dolls with gorgeous clothing, fairytale furniture, and accessories galore.

Set the stage for any adventure imaginable starring your favorite Stardust Classics characters.

Stardust
C L A S S I C S ™

If the postcard is missing, you can still get an iDolls catalog, featuring the Stardust Classics books and dolls. Send your name and address to:

iDolls
c/o Kid Galaxy, Inc.
104 Challenger Drive
Portland, TN 37148-1729

Or call our toll-free number:

1-800-410-1071

You can also request a catalog online. Visit us at our Website!

www.iDolls.com

Ask for Stardust Classics at your library or bookstore.